The Price of Passion

ARTEMIOS JOHN KORKIDIS

translated by DR. KATHERINE E. A. KORKIDIS

DORRANCE
PUBLISHING CO
EST. 1920
PITTSBURGH, PENNSYLVANIA 15238

Dorrance Publishing Co
585 Alpha Drive
Pittsburgh, PA 15238
Visit our website at *www.dorrancebookstore.com*

ISBN: 979-8-88683-532-8
eISBN: 979-8-88683-620-2

Although this book is written by Artemios John Korkidis I would like to dedicate this book to him. My father chose in his later years to write stories about his life and his experiences as a gift to his daughters and his grandchildren. Although written originally in Greek he asked that a translation be done so that all his grandchildren and their grandchildren could read it someday.

Thank you, Dad, for your constant love and always thinking of all of us. We are forever grateful for having you in our lives and now you will continue to live with us in our hearts and through your writings.

DR. KATHERINE E. A. KORKIDIS

PROLOGUE

Peter did not sleep all night. He tossed and turned to the right and then to the left continuously throughout the night until the dawn emerged. His guilty conscience, the source of his disturbance, tortured him. His thoughts of his future consumed him with doubt and dismay.

It is now summer, hot days ahead. The warm wind hammering the window did not help. He was alone. His wife and their three children are away, spending the summer months in Cyprus with extended family. The night before he spent the night in the arms of his beloved mistress. She was his first love of long ago. They found each other once again fortuitously and renewed their love. She was single, he was now married.

That night she confronted him, yet again, with an ultimatum. If they are to continue their relationship into the future, he must leave his wife, his family, and totally commit to her. But he could not. Yet, this time she made it very clear that she indeed would walk away from their relationship if he does not comply with her wishes. She is tired of his indecision. She no longer wishes to be merely the "other woman" but take on the role of his wife. She wants to be his wife now, not someday in the future.

They were separated many years prior by a decision made for him by his father. He still loved her and always regretted losing her. But now he had a wife in his life, a family. She too loved him and could not bear to lose him once again. Peter left her apartment that night earlier than usual and returned to his empty home. His thoughts were burdensome and so he fell into bed with the hope of sleeping, but sleep did not come. What can he do? How can he continue to have both women in his life and be faithful to each one.

The thought of losing his wife was paralyzing him. He would be devasted if he did lose her. He would not destroy his family especially with a wife that loves him unconditionally and with three angels that love and depend on their father. In his mind the dilemma was strong and, in some ways, induced by the devil himself. The dark and steep path that he was following would lead him to a dead end. It is dawn. He opens the window. In front of him he sees the bridge ready to greet him. A friend that knows him well since childhood when he played at her feet.

She greets the dawn of the day as she stands there dark, immobile filling up the view in the window. Her iron form reflects the ray of the morning sun temporarily blinding his tired eyes. The solution to his tragedy was unexpected but clear. Why did the solution not happen at night, when the Divine Judgment tormented the sinful body? Salvation was now before him. The beloved bridge was there for him. It will help him now. A dear friend that greets him every morning and bids him good night every night on his way from home to work and in return.

He made his decision. It is the only road to his salvation. He decided to wait for dinnertime. No one cares to see him. No one can stop him. This time he will pay a special visit to his beloved bridge. He will walk to meet her. It is not far. She is a good friend. He loves her and he knows she loves him. They are part of the same neighborhood. They share the same roots. She will listen to him as he tells her of his difficult situation. He is sure that it will help him to talk with her. She can bring him high up beyond the earth almost touching the sky. He is low right now near the earth, below her but she will raise him up. Of this, he is sure.

He opened the door and stood on the lower step so as not to be seen by his neighbors. He needed it to be darker before he could leave for this journey. He closed the door and proceed back into his house. He sat on the couch. His eyes roaming from the ceiling to the walls, to the furniture, everywhere, as if he were saying goodbye to a familiar place, yet somehow now seems unrecognizable to him.

Night has finally come bringing its dark veil. He picked up his umbrella and locked the door behind him. He headed on the road towards the bridge. She beckons him and he follows her call. He was tired and his knees were bending. He forced himself to stand up. He leaned against a wall for support and looked up at the sky. "God please help me", he cried out as he raised his eyes towards the sky. But the sky seemed still too far away. There was no answer. All was mute, indifferent, neither friend nor foe and he began to feel fear and lost. The stars were looking at him strangely and his heart froze.

"Where am I going? What will I do? Ah Yes, I forgot, the bridge is calling me. I am going to meet her tonight. Only she will save me ." And he started to walk towards her once again. The neighborhood was quiet, not a sound could be heard. No one was walking on his path. He was alone. He raised his head, and his eyes were amazed by the multicolor display that decorates the night coming from his beloved bridge. Two of the lights on the entrance illuminate the steps that will lead him to her final hug. And he goes up, goes up and up. Soon enough he disappears from view.

FROM THE TRANSLATOR:

By the time this book was translated, my father, Artemios (Art) Korkidis passed away. It was his request that I translate this particular book for his grandchildren. I too am an avid writer, and my only regret is that I did not finish his book before his death. He lived a long and wonderful life with a loving family, children, and grandchildren, and many many friends. The last few years of his life he was a prolific artist and writer. He had written four manuscripts that I am slowly translating and hope to add to his collection. His artistic work was scheduled for a showing at a local gallery in March 2020 but was postponed because of the pandemic.

My father was a gifted and highly talented man. He was a philosopher and an intellectual. He loved to learn and read, particularly politics, and was always there to help all who knew him. I am proud to be his daughter and give an audience to his many works. His legacy to all of us is his love of others, his thirst for education, and most of all his love for our natural world.

I miss him every day of my life.

Dr. Katherine E. A. Korkidis

CHAPTER ONE: THE BIRTH OF A SON

There was great joy in the home of Mr. Aristides. It had been ten years and the hopes that they would one day be a complete family were quickly disappearing. But today the news was what they were hoping for. Mrs. Hariklia will be bringing home in a few months a new member of their family. Someone long overdue and who they have been waiting for. She was 48 years of age, and her husband was thirty-nine. It might seem to most late to be a new mother but welcome just the same. The months seemed to pass quickly, and the anticipated day finally arrived. She was taken to Astoria Hospital for a son was to be born.

The family waited anxiously for the new arrival. And soon the son came. He opened his eyes and cried. The coming to this unknown world, a new little soul brought great joy to all. He was affectionately embraced by his parents who were thrilled and grateful for his arrival.

On the eastern side of Astoria, in the Greek community of Ditmars, somewhere on twenty-third street, there is the brick single family house of Aristides and Hariklia Triantafillou. Both of them from Cyprus, when they were first married, they were brought to America by Hariklia's big brother, Peter. He had been in America for many years. He worked hard and never had the opportunity to have a family. He was grateful to have his sister and brother-in-law join him. He had managed to become the owner of his own business, a restaurant that did very well.

The money he had saved allowed him to setup his sister and her husband in their own home. His brother in law joined him and worked as a cook in the restaurant while his sister tended the house. They spent eight years together happily. Peter was content and with the companionship of his family he was no longer lonely.

One night, peaceably, as all slept, Peter left them. He did not open his eyes in the morning. He passed during the night of a heart attack and left his family without his further guidance. Aristides continued running the restaurant. He was excellent as a businessman and the restaurant did very well.

The employees loved him, and all was perfect except that he and his wife wanted a child. A child just did not come easily to complement their happiness and love. But today was different. A child was born to Aristides and Hariklia Triantafillou. As the family returned to their home, they were greeted by their many friends, family, and neighbors anxious to meet the new treasure in the life of the Triantafillou family.

Every morning when Aristides would leave for work, he would tell his wife to keep her eye on the child while he was away. But his wife was even more protective than he would have been. She did not need the reminder but accepted it graciously. This treasure, long overdue. was to be highly guarded.

Happy was this middle aged father. His life, although later than planned now had purpose. Life was now worthwhile. He is no longer as tired as he was. Today he is invigorated as he walks on air with much joy in his heart, towards his restaurant. He opens the door, and he is greeted by his staff, all in place ready to serve his incoming clientele.

The setting of his kitchen was chosen by his brother in law, brother of his wife, who brought him to this kitchen. He became with time an excellent chef. The work was hard and promised long hours. Sweat would often encompass his body and face. But now he was not alone. He had two assistants, chefs, in the kitchen to fill those pans, pots, and plates. His ovens would accept his delicious food and cook those dishes for him. The grills were running searing the meat. The water was running to prepare the salads. All the components of the meal were ready at the same time and all his regulars were in place at their tables. Poor Aristides was doing this for twenty-three years. Hard and tedious work all those years. The years without hope and dreams.

Yet from this day on life would be different. One new young life was now immersed into the lives of this husband and wife. Dreams and hopes to illuminate their days and give strength and youth to the middle aged father, affection, and love to the heart of the mother. Mr. Aristides is no longer tired and forlorn.

He now walks quickly and with excitement every morning to work and finds himself almost running home at the end of the day. Sad to leave in the morning and ecstatic to return home in the evening. As he holds his child in his arms and gently puts his son to sleep, his dreams of a new life has now emerged to replace the bitter and frustrating ones of the past.

The infant is now four months old but not as yet named nor baptized. The infant needs a name and must be baptized. Possibly on a Monday. Aristides' restaurant was closed on Mondays to give rest to all the tired. This was the only day he was home to take care of other tasks that do not involve the restaurant. On this particular Monday two very close friends, Kostas and Maria came to celebrate their friends' happiness.

Kostas said, "now I think we have been given the opportunity to bond further with each other and go from friends to becoming in laws. Our very young daughter Argyro fell in love with your son and wants to baptize him." "Of course we can do this," responded Aristides. "We would love to have Argyro as his godmother. Further, when our son grows up, he will be thrilled to have such a young and beautiful young lady as his godmother, someone he will be proud of throughout his life." "What shall we call him? Have you chosen a name as yet?" asked Kostas. "Yes of course, replied Hariklia, we will call him John after my father in law."

"My wife, wait, said Aristides. The name of our son should be Peter, in reverence to your brother. This name gave us a home here and life. He shared all he had with us. He is the one I wish to honor. We owe him our life and our future." Hariklia wrapped her arms around her husband and held hands with her new potential in laws. The baptism will take place the following month, April, at the beginning of the month, before Easter, on that Sunday, at the Greek Orthodox Church of St. Demetrius in Astoria.

All was ready from the warm water in the baptismal font, to the priest and chants of his cantors, to the baptismal dress for their angel, to the preparation of this infant's godmother by her parents. The baptism begins. The priest rolls up his sleeves and takes the child from the parents. He proceeds to dip the child into the water, as you would dip a biscuit in your coffee. He immerses the child entirely, body and head, into the water two additional times, ignoring the crying infant. This way he abided by the teachings of the Orthodox faith.

The godmother standing next to the priest is ready to remove the wet clothes of the infant and wraps him with a clean white sheet. She takes the child from the wet hands of the representative of God. She acts like a young lady rather than a child as she holds the little creature tightly in her arms as she would her dolls. Her mother is by her side to guide and help her. "Are you able to hold him, my child," asks her mother. "Yes, mama I can," she answers. "He is not heavy. I am so very happy," she replied. And so finishes the sacrament of Baptism and with the completion of this sacrament so does the original sin of this new Christian with the name Peter. His first sin, his first suffering are gone. The Holy Spirit from this point on offers him life and guides him.

All the guests walked from the church to the nearby avenue called Broadway in Astoria. Astoria is a neighborhood in the western portion of New York City in the borough of Queens. It is the center of Greek-American businesses in this area. Broadway is the heart of Astoria, one of New York's largest Greek communities, and often called "Greek Town." The 1960s saw a large increase of a

Greek population from mainland Greece, and after 1974, there was an influx of Greeks from particularly Cyprus.

This cultural imprint can be seen in the numerous Greek restaurants, tavernas, bakeries, and cafes, as well as several Greek Orthodox churches. St. Demetrius is one of those churches. The baptism was to be celebrated in a large hall affiliated with one of those restaurants on Broadway. The baptized new addition to the Greek Orthodox community was placed close to his godmother.

The many other guests were seated around the decorated tables enjoying their favorite dishes and music. At the same table sat both set of parents, dear friends from their first years in their second homeland. All were joyful and happy. They remember and knew how to celebrate the joys of their homeland, which once abroad become important to teach each generation to come.

"To a good life for our little sprout." "To a good life that we can all be proud of." The glasses full of Greek nectar clung together as an accompaniment to the music. The dances of Cyprus were expressed on the dance floor by those from the homeland, who did not forget their roots. Time has flown and the godmother of this infant Peter has finished her elementary and middle school studies and is now entering high school. Every afternoon after her classes she would attend Greek School at St. Demetrius for three hour sessions after school to become fluent in the language of Modern Greek. It was important to her parents that she could read and speak the language of her ancestors.

It is spring and the sun is warm. The sky is a uniform blue. Astoria Park is situated at the foot of the beautiful Triborough Bridge and is a 60-acre public park in the Astoria neighborhood of Queens in New York City. The Triborough bridge is a well- traveled and recognized thoroughfare between the areas of Astoria and the Bronx. The Park is situated on the eastern shore of the Hell Gate, a strait of the East River, between Ditmars Boulevard to the north and Hoyt Avenue to the south.

The Triborough and Hell Gate Bridges respectively pass over the park's southern and northern sections. The Park lies on a hill that gently travels down to a waterway known as the East River with boats and speedboats traversing it. At the edges along the blanket of green you can find trees and flowers and benches for the weary. Rest for the bodies of many passers-by and neighbors. A magical, vivid, and invaluable image that alternated its colors from day to night.

The young godmother loves the park especially its vicinity to her home and to the home of her godchild who is now three years old. "Excuse me Mrs. Hariklia, can I take Peter for a walk in the park?" "My child, of course you can. I will get him ready to go." In a few minutes, the child was in his stroller and ready to leave with his godmother. "Argie, please watch over the child." "Of course I will. Please do not worry."

At the park, the children are playing on the grass. The adults are walking on the trails. The elderly are sitting on the benches. The spring sun provides all both with warmth and light hugging this happy crowd that has wandered out to greet her. The two children, a fifteen year old godmother and her three years old godchild are playing on the grass with their ball and their laughter permeates through the air.

The mother of her only child worries each time his godmother takes him away from their home. With various excuses she tries to stop them from exiting. But the little one loves the park. The road, the cars that are racing, the dangers they represent were enough to terrify her. Most of the time she tries to accompany them to the park and stays with them. The bridge high and imposing in the mind of the child offers an image of a great God that he must fear but knows that it protects him.

Young Peter loves the outdoors. Especially the sunny days of spring and the warm days of summer. His godmother would usually accompany him. But his godmother was now gone. Having finished high school in Astoria she had started the university far from home. Her life had changed. New gatherings, friends, and companions, she forgot her godchild. His mother took over as his companion to take him to his favorite place, the park.

"Mana, where is my godmother? Why does she not want me anymore?" "My child, your godmother will always want you. She will never forget you. For now she is not here with us. She is in a place far away to learn and extend her education." The summer evenings when the heat had subsided, Aristides and Hariklia would take their only child to the park. There under the shade of the trees and the cool breezes coming off the river, they could admire the beauty of the night.

Years go by, the children get older as do the parents. The circle of life continues its pace forward. Never backwards. The young godmother is no longer in her early youth. She has grown up. She finished her university studies in California and became a physician. She met another young doctor and they wed. She too was an only child not unlike her godson. She left her home of her youth to a new life and brought her parents with her. With the relocation of the parents, Aristides and Hariklia lost their friends and were now alone in the old neighborhood.

Peter is finishing up his senior year at William Collin Bryant HS in Astoria. He has a girlfriend, a fellow student, a non-Greek girl of Jewish descent. He loves her very much, very much. "Watch over our son, my dear wife. He is of an impressionable age. I do not want him to get involved with a girl that is not of the same background. I see everywhere such relationships happening. When the time comes, I will know what to do." "Do not be so concerned, my husband. I am carefully watching our son. They are only friends, not boyfriend and girlfriend."

Peter knows his parents' concerns. The constant monitoring by his mother disappoints him. It makes him angry. He does not like the constant response of "no." "Do not go here or there." All those "no's," although done out of protection for their only son and certainly out of love, were restrictive for Peter and eliminated all choices and freedoms. Yet his parents love him very much, they are his biggest fans. Being an only child, Peter does not have siblings to share in this deep love and worship.

This devotion and constant surveillance was acceptable to Peter when he was young. However he is no longer a child but a teen. He understands their concerns but his wants their behavior to end. As a teen his desires and choices are changing. His transition into a young adult is taking place. Yet his parents were steadfast in their desire to monitor his every move. It is not unusual that parents with only one child would be focused on their child's wellbeing. They cannot and should not leave their side.

They must survey all their child's choices. They must constantly monitor them and protect them but in doing so they limit the ability of this teen to develop in an independent young adult. Part of growing up and becoming an adult is making mistakes, as long as they are not serious, irreversible mistakes and to learn from those mistakes. By constantly monitoring Peter his parents stunted his emotional and intellectual growth.

Peter is in love, deep love. He sees her as the perfect woman. No other girl could fill him with such love and admiration, with such happiness. He wanted to marry her and believed that by doing so he would be transformed into someone as perfect as she. She is his soulmate and fills his soul with beauty. Her presence in his life fills his heart with song.

The love he feels for this young girl cannot be hidden. He hugs his mother and father and shows his love for them. His parents are concerned and cannot understand this sudden good will from their son. "What is it that makes you so very happy?" Peter's father asks after dinner. "I am happy because I am finishing my schooling and I would like to work with you. I miss working with you."

During the years Peter attended high school he would often take the train in the afternoon to the Bronx to help his father by working in the family's restaurant. "Why work with me? Do you not wish to go to college to become something else? Maybe a doctor or a lawyer. These are careers not jobs and are much lighter work. Working and running a restaurant is very tedious work. You work long hours and have little or no time to enjoy your life. Why not follow in the footsteps of your godmother that chose a career in medicine. Do you not wish to follow her example?"

"Let this go, Father, do not be concerned. We will see for I do not know." The son was afraid that if he waited for another year until after he finished high school, he might lose his beloved. He might go in one direction and she in a different direction. Who knows what will happen. They might forget each other. He does not want to lose her. He needs to hold on to her but how – only if he marries her today. He believes that he should approach his mother with his situation.

"Mama, I lied to my father that my happiness as of late is linked to the possibility of working with him once I graduate. The truth is that I am in love. This gives me the happiness I cannot seem to hide." "My child, what are you saying? I cannot fathom that you my young child is in love and is happy because of it. I know that your only friends and constant companions are George and Paul. They are wonderful young men, your fellow classmates. I see them with you every day. That is why I did not worry about you. Now you have made me worry. I am afraid of what your father will do once he finds out."

"Mama, I have told you my secret because I know you will understand. I do not dare say this to my father. He will not understand."

"Yes, he will not understand and I was to plan your future. He gave me this responsibility."

"But Mama, what can I do? I love that girl with all my heart. She is so beautiful. Like an angel with blonde hair and a lovely face. Once you see her, meet her, you will love her. I am thinking of bringing her to our home so you and she can meet."

"Please do not do this, my child. Wait until I speak with your father first." "Okay, Mama, but do not linger. I do not wish to lose her. I wish to marry her." "My son, my child, what has possessed you. You are too young to be thinking of marriage." "Mama, I will wait."

It was just now that Mrs. Hariklia finally realized why her son did not come straight home from school after his daily classes. He would tell her he was with his friends. His friends were part of the lie and help cover for him. It was during that time that her son was with his girlfriend. The discovery that Peter had a girlfriend upset the mother. How will she be able to tell her husband. She was afraid, very afraid. Every evening when her husband would return home, she would greet him with a melancholy face.

"Wife, is there something wrong? I can see that you are upset and have been so over the last 2-3 days. I did not bother to ask you then but is something wrong?" "No, Aristides. Nothing is wrong." "Then why are you not as happy as Peter that he will join me and help me at the restaurant? His happiness is great, and he cannot wait until his schooling is done."

Mrs. Hariklia thought of saying something. The opportunity came without her prompting it. Yet she felt like she lost her voice. She swallowed her saliva with difficulty. She tried to speak two or three times, but no voice emerged. She swallowed her saliva again, but a sound could not be heard. She sat on the sofa and signaled her husband to come and sit next to her. She forced her voice.

"My husband, our son is happy that he will be able to help you, that is true, but he is even more happier because he is in love with a fellow classmate." The words exited from her mouth very quickly. She could not contain them. They were choking her. "What did you say? I do not understand. Please repeat what you said. Our son is in love, how, with whom?"

"No, not really in love. Simply the girl and our son are friends and classmates. They spend time together and I wish to invite her to our home to get to know her." "It is your fault that our son chose this path. It is your fault that you did not realize what he does at school. It is your fault that your eyes have been closed. Unless of course you are encouraging his actions behind my back. I am angry with you, not with him."

"Aristide why am I at fault? Our son has kept his actions secret. I saw him with his friends every day. How was I to know that he was involved with a young lady. He never told me. He finally told me yesterday. He was too intimidated to tell you. It was easier for him to tell me. When he told me I was hesitant to bring it up. Today I did tell you. It is not right for me to know what is happening with our son and to not share it with you."

"I am very upset. That is why he is not interested in pursuing his education further, because he is in love. Love makes one blind and an idiot. He is not at fault. We are at fault for not seeing this before all went bad. Maybe the communication gap is between us. Maybe we need to examine what is happening to us." "My husband, Peter would like to bring her here so we can meet her. What shall we do? Do you wish to meet her?"

"What did you say? No, absolutely no, I will not do so. Also I do not wish to see my son any longer. I cannot tolerate someone who has secrets. We were together every day, why did he not talk to me about it." "Because he did not dare to do so. He knows you are very strict. He was scared of your reaction. Yes, he was very scared." "Does he not realize that he is not in a position to pursue such a relationship? He is too young for such a coupling. Who is she? Is she Greek?"

"I do not know. He did not tell me. Aristides, my opinion is that we allow him to bring her here. This way we can find out who she is and anything else we observe with our own eyes. He is blinded by romantic love and desire. Romantic love blinds one from seeing what is real. When we first met was it eros? I do not know but if it was it developed into love. Eros passes away with time, but love lasts. It is a matter of urgency. It is like a bad disease such as cancer, if you do not catch it in its early stages you will die. Therefore we must hurry to prevent eros from developing into love."

"I did not know I had such a wise woman next to me whose thoughts were so detailed and accurate." "You are so right. Tell him to bring her here." The son was waiting for an answer each coming day. He is anxious. He has no patience. "My Mama, come so I can kiss you? You are the best mother in all the world."

Peter is enthusiastic. He did not believe such a resolution. He did not understand why his father gave his consent so readily. It was not like him. He expected anger, a more intense noncooperative reaction. He did not expect his father to accept his request. But things appear different, strange. As he thought about it, he realizes he must be cautious in his enthusiasm. Maybe his father has something in store for him. Something he does not expect.

He purposely delayed returning home. His father goes to bed early and leaves at early dawn for work. He never sees him at home. He does see him at the restaurant when he goes to help his father. From the moment he confided his secret to his mother he has been avoiding him and has not met him at work. He is afraid, if his mother told his father his secret, of his father's disposition. Now that his dad knows everything the son is ready for a confrontation.

Today is Sunday. Every Sunday Peter spends all day with his friends. At least that is what he told his mother to explain his absence. But now, Mrs. Hariklia knew where and with whom her beloved son would spend his time. Even knowing all, the mother would wait up for him every night. She would not go to sleep until her only son returned to and entered their home.

"Mama, I have one concern. It appears to me odd that my father would have accepted so easily bringing this girl to our home. I would never have imagined that he would have welcomed her. I could only imagine his anger and that he would have killed me if I did bring her to our home. That is why I am afraid to speak with him. What happened? What did you tell him?" "I spoke to him logically and he understood. Do not worry. Bring the girl tomorrow. You did not tell me her name. What is her name?" "Anthea, her name is Anthea." "Anthea, beautiful. Tomorrow evening we will expect the arrival of Anthea."

Peter is happy tonight. His father has agreed to meet his beloved. He was mistaken with the idea that his father would deny to meet her. "I am sure now I was wrong about my father. My father is a good man and loves me. If I knew that this would have been his response, I would have told him directly about my situation. I do not know why I feared him."

He was anxious to awaken so he could run and meet his love. "Anthea, my parents are waiting for us this evening to meet you." "I am ready, Peter. I too would like to meet them. If I was to judge them based on you, I would say they are very nice. I am afraid that all might not be the way you wish them to be. Do not dismiss their concerns. We are not really ready for marriage. That is obvious except you cannot see it."

"I see it with my eyes. The eyes of love. I do not wish to lose you. I want to marry you, now, this instant." "All I am saying is that I am afraid. That is why I did not as yet invite you to meet my parents. I think it is too early to tell them about us. I believe it was premature to tell your parents. Let us go now and may God Bless you."

Peter's family is ready. The home is also ready. They are anxious to meet this person their son is bringing to their home. The mother, Mrs. Hariklia, is at the door ready to greet the lovers. The son is ebullient. His face is happy. The girl is nervous. Her hands are trembling as they meet the hands of her future mother in law.

They continue into the house. The father stands up from his seat. He welcomes the future bride. The young lady is very beautiful. The son told his mother the truth as to the young girl's beauty and how she would love her too once she saw her.

Mr. Aristides led the couple to the living room. Peter took the girl's hand and they sat down on the sofa. Mrs. Hariklia happily laid on the small table a tray of glasses filled with orange juice then sat next to her husband across from the lovebirds. The parents do not look happy. The girl is nervous. The son is anxious. The father begins the interrogation.

"Your name is Anthea." "Yes, that is correct." "I understand from Peter that you are fellow classmates." "Yes, that is correct. We attend the same high school. We met there."

"Do you have family here in Astoria? Do you live nearby?" "No, we live in Sunnyside. We have a house there." "Yes, I know it, it is close by. That is why you can attend William Cullen Bryant High School." "Yes, you are correct."

"Do you live with your parents?" "Yes." "Do you have siblings?" "Yes, two brothers and one sister. All younger than me." "What does your father do for a living?" "He owns and manages a Delicatessen in Sunnyside. In our neighborhood." "Oh so I see that he too is a businessman. We have much in common."

The father and the young bride continue to talk. The son is studying his father's face for any reaction to the answers given. The mother is in the kitchen preparing food. The son leaves the discussion and hurries to the kitchen to speak with his mother. "Mama, what do you think of the young woman? Isn't she as beautiful as I told you she would be?"

"Yes, my child. She is beautiful and appears to be from a good family." After the inquisition, they all move to the dining room table to enjoy the delicious meal prepared by Mrs. Hariklia. The questions to get to know the young girl had finished. Dark is setting in and the young girl rose from the table. "I am so sorry to disrupt this wonderful evening, but I must leave now. My parents will be worried if I am late."

"Of course, my dear girl. You are a wonderful child, and you are concerned about your parents," answered Mr. Aristides. "Thank you for the wonderful company and hospitality." (It is important to note that the conversation this evening was all in English. The young potential bride did not speak Greek.)

All walk towards the door. The son takes the hand of the girl, and they exit the home. "I will not be late. I will walk Anthea to her home." "Take a taxi my child," answers his mother.

The door closes behind them. Mr. Aristides proceeds to return to the living room. He sits on the sofa pensively. Mrs. Hariklia sits next to him. "Well, how do you see the situation, my husband?" "Are you asking me how I see the situation. Well I see it black and bleak. The young girl is nice and easily liked. I do not know more beyond that. What concerns me right now is that my son is too young to be that deeply in love." "If you only knew that he wishes to marry her now. That is what he told me. He is in a hurry to marry her. He wants to do so now before he graduates. He is afraid of losing her."

"Is that right, accounting without a plan. I believe that are son is moving much too fast. Do not worry I will find the way to stop him. If at least the girl was Greek, which I do not believe is true, we could have postponed the wedding to a later time. I asked her many questions except I did not ask her directly about her ethnicity. I did not think it was appropriate. Yet I am sure she is not Greek. If she were, she would have said at least one Greek word during our conversation. What do you think?"

"I agree with you. When he returns tonight, I will ask him about her ethnicity and from where her family originated." "Okay, I must go to sleep now. I must wake up early tomorrow morning. Ask him to come by the restaurant in the afternoon."

"Aristide, I beg you do not tell him what you told me. I am afraid we will lose him if we do not accommodate him. Please wait. We will find the time for both of us to talk to him. Did you not see how he acts. He is crazy about her."

"Yes, you are right. Please do not forget to ask him about her ethnicity. So we know. I am telling you now. If this young lady has no affiliation with Greece whether we lose him or not, all his plans for further education will be ruined." The young son returned home late, as always. His mother is waiting for him, as always.

"Well, Mama, I understand you liked the young lady very much. I could see it in your face because I know you. You cannot fool me. I know you very well. My father did not seem to have the same response as you. The questions he asked her sounded like an interrogation of a prosecutor addressing a criminal. I am being honest with you. Anthea was upset by his interrogation. I was embarrassed and upset as well by such an interrogation by my father. Anthea likes you but not my father. She did not tell me directly, but I could tell. She easily showed her admiration for you when she said, "your mother is a wonderful woman. She chose not to say a word about my father."

"The truth is that you are still too young for this situation. Maybe that is the reason your father acted the way he did. Neither I nor your father have anything bad to say about the girl. She was perfectly respectful in her behavior towards us. Tell me about her family. Have you gone to her home? Did you meet her parents? You know we are Greek, and you are of Greek descent. What is she? What is her ethnicity? Do you know?"

"Yes, her parents are Jewish. She is of Jewish descent. But that does not matter. We are all the same in this world." "Oh, really!"

The mother felt as if she was struck by lightning. The bolt lighted up her face and she lost her voice. "What has happened to you, Mama? You do not look well." "My son I am okay. Forget about it. Your father has asked that you go by the restaurant this afternoon if you wish to do so."

"I will not be able to do so today. I do not have the time. We have to stay at the school until late. Maybe tomorrow unless he needs to talk with me today. What do you think, Mama?"

"I do not know. Forget about it. Do not go today and we will see about tomorrow."

The mother regretted that she told her son to go to the restaurant. She did not think it through when she told him to go because if his father asked him about the girl's ethnicity, he would have answered, Jewish. Once his father heard that response he would explode. No, no do not go today she told him. Luckily, the son could not go. She needed to discuss this with her husband first to calm him down. God only knows what a catastrophe this will become, and no one will survive.

Mrs. Hariklia was trembling from head to foot. How will she be able to tell her husband that the prospective bride is Jewish. She was afraid. But she must tell him. He asked her to inquire about this. Not only is she not Greek, which her husband was convinced she was a non-Greek. He understood that she was not Greek, but a non-Greek and of the Jewish faith, he would never accept that. She was concerned that the latter would cause him to become vividly upset. How can she tell him the terrible news. "Woe is me," she said with chattering teeth. "How will I survive once I tell him. He will really kill me."

In the evening, Mr. Aristides came home tired and eager to hear what his wife learned about the girl. "Were you able to get our descendant to tell you what I asked about?" "Yes, my husband, I was able to do so. But first come and rest and eat the meal I prepared for you. It is your favorite. We can talk later." "Alright. I will first wash up."

As he finished up in the bathroom and proceeded to the dining room Mrs. Hariklia found the opportunity to change the subject of their conversation. She was afraid, afraid of the outcome. More so, she was concerned that her husband might have a stroke once she tells him about the faith of this young girl. Yet she had no other choice. As they finished dinner, she took her husband by the hand and led him to the sofa. They sat down.

"Aristides are you alright? Are you feeling, okay? What I am about to tell you do you promise me not to let it upset you?" "What is wrong with you, wife. What are you afraid to tell me? That the girl is not Greek, I already know and understand that. I told you that yesterday. She is a non-Greek." "You are right, my husband, she is not Greek."

"Well, what is she, Italian, Spanish, Irish, what?" "I need you here." Mrs. Hariklia lost her voice. She became dizzy and fainted. "What happened to you. Your face is very pale. Sit here and I will run to get you a glass of water." The wife opened her lips and began to slowly sip the water. She took a deep breath and opened her lips once more this time to take in a larger drink.

"Holy Mary, what is it that frightens you so that you cannot tell me. Why are you so afraid that I would kill you?" "Aristides, the girl is not only foreign to being Greek but has a different religion, she is Jewish." It was Aristides turn to fall back into his seat in shock. The veins in his head became pronounced and he appeared to lose consciousness.

"Is this the truth or are you telling me lies." "It is the truth, Aristides. Please settle down. We will find a way to correct this situation. I promise you." "We are not only changing our ethnicity but also our religion. Is this where we are? Is this where our only son has taken us? I do not wish to ever see him again. He is never to enter our home again."

Staggering and leaning against the wall for support, the father tried to walk. His wife hugged him and helped him to bed, afraid that something severe could happen to her husband.

The son returned home that evening. The mother told him of his father's reaction when he found out that the girl was not Greek. The son said angrily, "I did not expect such rejection by my own parents.

You are no longer my parents. You are strangers to me. I asked you to be happy for me and you denied me such happiness. I am leaving. I do not wish to see you ever again."

"My son, why are you saying such things." The son did not answer his mother. He opened the door and disappeared into the darkness. His mother dropped onto the sofa and immersed her head into her two hands. Her eyes are running continuously. She falls asleep from exhaustion.

It is now morning and Mr. Aristides was getting ready to leave for his restaurant. He was surprised to see his wife asleep on the sofa. He awoke her and she told him all that had happened the night before. He left for work with a heavy heart.

The son did not come home that night, nor the next night, nor the next. The mother stayed up waiting for him. His father was upset, silent and narrowminded. He has deep love for his son and does not wish to lose him. He could not work as he did before. He feels an emptiness in his heart. The mother is worried. She begins to call all his friends to see if he is staying with them. Her son finally calls on the third day.

"What is it you want, Mother?" "My child, where have you been for so many days?" "I was with Paul." "What will his parents say that you left your home and are living there? I am embarrassed." "Well then, I am not embarrassed. It does not concern you where I am living."

"Peter, I am begging you. Please come home." "If I return, will he accept that I marry the girl I love? What does he say?" "Who is he? Your father?" "Yes, him." "Your father cannot live without you. But he cannot accept you marrying a Jewish girl that does not share our religious beliefs." "Then I will not return. Tell my father to forget me."

The son slammed the phone down. The mother held the quiet phone to her ear for a while longer. Eventually she placed it back in its place. She collapsed in a chair near her with a pale face and tear filled eyes. It is evening and the husband returns home with agony in his soul.

"Did our son call or come today?" "No, Aristides, he did not come. He called and told me if we did not agree that he is to marry the woman that he loves, he will never return. He will return only if we change our minds and agree. "Okay then, my wife, it does not matter. So be it. Let him to never return."

"Come eat." "No, I am not hungry." "I am very tired, and I will go to get some rest."

Mrs. Hariklia took her husband to his bed. Not that much longer she too joined him in bed. She noticed that her husband was sleeping on his back with his mouth open and breathing heavily. She tried to move him, but he did not respond. He would not wake up. She panicked and thought he was dying. She called 911 and medical assistance arrived in ten minutes. He was taken to the hospital, diagnosis, heart attack. She went with him in the ambulance and stayed by his side in the hospital. Her only thoughts at this moment were to die. She did not wish to live any longer.

The next day she called her son's friend, Paul from the hospital room, to ask him to tell her son Peter that his father is in the hospital in serious condition. It was less than six minutes and Peter entered his father's hospital room. His father lay there motionless with his eyes closed and an oxygen mask on his face. His mother was sitting next to him with tear drenched eyes.

"What happened, mother. How did this happen?" "I do not know. It was in the evening that he had the heart attack. He had much sadness, and you have to know why." The son understood his mother's accusation. He grabbed his head with both his hands and started to pound his head into the wall. He embraced his unconscious father. He fell onto his knees in front of his bitter mother with the guilt felt by a murderer. He had killed his father, the reason, his preoccupation with being in love. He hugged his mother. Her tears ran down her face. He lifted her up from the chair and took her with him. Slowly they descend the steps and with care he held her as they exited the hospital. He called a taxi and they returned home together. He hugged her and sat her down on the sofa and sat down next to her.

"Mother, please forgive me. I am responsible for everything. I was arrogant. I was thinking of myself only. I was selfish and did not care about how much others loved me. I am asking God to heal my father. Never again will I upset him nor you. You are both my loving parents. My parents are the best people in this world, and I will always remember this."

He made something for his mother to eat and then he put her to bed to catch up on all the sleep she had lost the night before. He stayed by her side the entire night. The next morning he got ready to return to his classes. "Mother, please do not go to the hospital today by yourself. Wait for me to return and we will go together." "Okay my child, I will wait for you."

In the face of this tragic event, he almost lost his father who loved him very much and more so that this was his own fault, he reflected on what was to come. He must choose between the young girl that he loves and his deep love for his parents. He realized now that he could not have both loves. He would have to choose. He asked to meet his young lady at school and told her about his father's sudden and serious illness and much more.

The young girl understood. She did not say anything, just listened to Peter. She realized that their love was no longer possible. It withstood the father's initial rejection but not his illness. She could sense by what he told her that he no longer felt the same, he no longer loved her with the same intensity. She was not prepared for such a change in him. All was lost for now but maybe one day it could change. One could only hope.

It is June, last exams were taken, and graduation was done. The young lovers are together for one last time. Soon they will go their separate ways. Peter wanted so much to marry Anthea that he was willing to give everything up, even the love of his parents. Yet after his father's illness all had changed. It was as if he was struck by the lightening of this new reality. The possible loss of his father touched his soul and redefined his priorities and his future.

CHAPTER TWO: PETER BECOMES A YOUNG MAN

It has been two weeks in the hospital for Mr. Aristides. He was finally well enough to return home. His doctors told him to be careful not to get over tired and not allow stress in his life. Mrs. Hariklia loves her husband and watches out for him. Peter, their only son loves his father. He is grateful to God for allowing his father to live and to continue to be in his life.

So Peter has now completed his secondary education. He has his high school diploma in hand, but he must go beyond high school. Yet he feels he needs to work with his father in the restaurant. "Father, from now on I will take over managing the restaurant. I would like you to rest to become completely well."

"Peter, I am fine. I do not want you to stop your future studies because of me. I do not wish for you to follow in my footsteps. I do not want you to live in a kitchen amongst the pots and pans. I want you to work towards a professional career."

"Father, I do not wish to continue my studies. I do not like the idea of pursuing higher education and would prefer to become a chef. I love the idea of feeding the world. I love what you do and wish to follow in your footsteps. Starting tomorrow I plan to be at the restaurant from morning to night. Mr. John will train me in anything I need to learn. There is no need for you to tire yourself any longer. You have done so for so long. You can now retire, stay home, and spend time with my mother."

"We will see. I have worked all my life. If I now must retire, then life is not worth living."

"Please get well and then we will see." At eighteen years of age, Peter was ready to work on his future. He obtained his driver's license and he learned to drive his father's car to work. He likes his job and is happy.

Meanwhile his young lady after finishing high school said good-bye to her beloved. She decided to pursue her higher education far from home ultimately to create a professional career unlike Peter's goals. Her family remained in Sunnyside.

Peter is determined to learn the restaurant business. Between his devotion to his work and his parents he is very busy. Yet on occasion his mind goes back to the memory of his past love. His soul often feels empty by absence of his beloved. On multiple occasions he has passed by her home in the hope that he will see her, but to no avail. He thought about stopping in and ask her family about her and where she might be, but he does not dare to do so. He tries to forget; he needs to forget and move on with his life. So he walks away.

Mr. Aristides feels very well. His health is improving every day. Two to three times a week his son brings him to the restaurant. He does not wish to see his father depressed because he is sitting at home, yet he does not want him to work. His father has just turned 66 years of age and is getting his pension. Retirees should not be working. The young should work in their place. In his youth his father too worked hard to relieve others that had retired. This is indeed the 'circle of life'. We are young and work hard until our retirement then offer our experience to the young that replace us.

Meanwhile at home Mr. Aristides and Mrs. Hariklia being alone exchange their thoughts about their only son. "Hariklia, tell me how you see our son. Have you noticed anything about him." "In what way, Aristides? What is it you are trying to say?" "In reference to women, do you think he has forgotten the Jewish girl, or does he want her still? Is he interested in someone else? Has he spoken to you about this topic?" "No, he has not spoken to me about anyone. Once I did ask him about the Jewish girl he was crazy about, do you remember, he said he is no longer interested in her. He learned that she left but has no idea where she is living." "Are you sure or are your eyes closed as per before?" "No, I am sure. This time my eyes are open."

"Alright then, let me tell you what I have in mind. I believe you will agree with me. Let us try to get him married through our intervention before he finds another girl on his own. I will write to my niece in Cyprus to find a nice girl from our village. Then we will convince him to accompany us on a vacation to the island so he can see our homeland without telling him our real purpose. What do you think of my plan?"

"I agree and we should do it." "Good, let us wait a little bit longer until he becomes twenty years old. But watch him so as not to lose him. You are responsible, do not forget. Know that I will not forgive you this time as I did in the past."

Mr. Aristides is looking forward to his son growing up to become twenty years old so he can implement his plan before his son finds a way to ruin it. He felt it was a dangerous time until his son turns twenty. If his son gets involved once again with another girl, his plan would be useless. At this age he is still too young to have a family. It is more logical for someone older closer to thirty years old. But the situation here is different. There is a danger in waiting so he has hired two trusted individuals to watch over his son. His employee from the restaurant, John, and his wife, Mrs. Hariklia.

Peter is not the least bit interested in a relationship at this time. He is focused on succeeding as a business man and growing his business. "Father, why is the store next door empty? Who owns it?" "Why do you ask, Peter?" "Maybe we could buy it and expand our restaurant into the new space." "Why do we need to expand our current space?" "Father, you are not living in the real world. Our current business needs expansion and as such more space. More space means more customers. I know what I am doing."

"Alright, Peter, whatever you think is best. I am no longer the manager, you are. Us older men are set in our ways, whereas the young bring in new ideas." "Father do not be offended. I do not want to offend you. You are the one that opened this business and kept it alive for many years. But you have to know that times change. Today there are other opportunities and demands. If I have any experience in business, it is because I learned from you. You have been my teacher."

"Peter I am only joking with you. Did you not understand it to be so? You are correct and your ideas are good. I agree. Do what you think is best. I am with you in this plan. Tomorrow I will try to find the owner of the space next door and see if he is interested in selling it. I know who he is."

"Alright Father, thank you." Mr. Aristides found the man that owned the neighboring space. They were neighbors and friends for seven years. The store sold women's dresses and handbags. It has been vacant for one year. He had relocated to another state, New Jersey, and only returned on rare occasions. Today was one of those days.

He is now retired and has health issues. Mr. Aristides called him and told him he was interested in purchasing the space if it was for sale. He reminded him that they were neighbors. The owner remembered him. The man told him that he was interested in renting the space, but his illness intervened, and the deal did not go through. He had not thought about selling it, but it sounded good. He promised that he would answer him tomorrow. They exchanged telephone numbers. Mr. Aristides is waiting. His son is happy.

The answer came in two days. He agreed to sell his space. He gave the phone number of his son to communicate with Mr. Aristides the details of the sale. "Peter we will be buying the space next door. You are indeed lucky. You will work out the details with the son of the owner. Here is his telephone number."

Mr. Aristides was very happy that is son is interested in the success of the business and does not have time for other dangerous social endeavors. In the end the father does not care about his son's plans regarding the restaurant. All he is concerned with is that his son does not marry before his twentieth year. He waits impatiently for his plan to come to fruition.

His niece in Cyprus has come through. She found what he was looking for, a beautiful and perfect young lady of similar age to his unsuspecting son. Mr. Aristides and Mrs. Hariklia are both anxious to organize their trip and they decided to include their son in the arrangements.

"Peter, do you know that your mother and I were not born in America. We came from a beautiful island very far from here called Cyprus." "Yes, Father, I know. You have told me many times." "Peter, yes, I have mentioned it many times but today I am telling you again. Do you know why?" "Why" "Because I want to return to the place of my birth one more time before I die." "Father, you should go. There is nothing stopping you from going."

"No one is stopping me, but I do not wish to go alone." "Then take mama with you." "It is not about your mother only. I would like all of us to go together." "If you go just with my mother that should be fine. Why do you need me to come?" "Peter, you have never been there. It is so beautiful. You will like it very much so much so you will not wish to leave from there."

"Yes father, you are correct. You are retired and free to go wherever you wish to go. I have to work and cannot take the time off." "Okay then I will not go. If we cannot go all together, why should I go." "But Father, who will take care of the restaurant?"

"Leave it in the hands of John, my trusted employee. He will do the same job each of us would do. It would be as if we were managing the restaurant. This way we could go wherever we would like and stay as long as we would wish to." "Okay, I have to think about it. I must repeat, go with Mom. It is the same thing."

Peter's parents decided not to discuss the trip again with their son. He is focused on the restaurant, and they do not wish to create problems. As planned, Peter succeeded in buying the neighboring space at a good price. He combined the two spaces and completed the necessary renovations. He rearranged the staff and added more waiters to accommodate the additional tables. The new tables were filled, and the profits expanded with the new space. His focus on the success of the business silenced Mr. Aristides and Mrs. Hariklia.

The winter passed, the spring came, and the summer is not far behind. Peter remembered the trip his father mentioned more than one year ago. "Father, what do you plan to do? Will you go in the summer to Cyprus?" "No, Peter, we will not go. Since you do not wish to go with us, we will stay here. It is not important that I die without seeing my homeland."

The son became upset with his father's words. He realized that his refusal to go with his parents was like a knife embedded in his father's heart. The hurt in their eyes convinced him that he must go. He had no other choice. He did not wish to hurt him further. "Okay, Father, I will go with you." "No, my child, let it go. I do not wish to disrupt your work. I just will not go."

"No, Father, we will go together this coming summer. But only for one month. If that is okay. I agree with you Father that John is wonderful, and we can trust him to take care of the restaurant while we are away."

"I am very grateful my child. You are for me my world." The parents were unhappy at first even though their plan had taken on form. They were not truthful with their only son but for now they decided to go forward with their plan just the same. The parents and son were ready for their trip to Cyprus. A taxi took them to the airport. The plane took off for their destination. One night in the air and by the next day at noon they set foot on the island of Aphrodite. At the Nicosia International Airport, Aristides' niece and her family welcomed them with open arms.

It has been many years since they last met. The faces might have changed as age set in, but the joy of reunion was deeply embedded in their souls. Peter has never seen such a world before, very different from the one he was living in. He looked up at a blue and clear sky with beauty of this island surrounding him. He was shown the true presence of summer. He was happy to be experiencing this beauty and the promise of meeting his family.

"Welcome to our home," was heard said by all present. Hugs and kisses followed from his niece's family on Mr. Aristides' side. "We are blessed by God to see you as we return from America." "We are indeed blessed by God. We are quite joyous that you have come to visit us. We awaited this visit with much anticipation. To be able also to meet Peter for the first time, our cousin is an even greater blessing."

"We waited to come until Peter had become a young adult. We came mostly for him to meet his family and learn about his roots." "Peter, what do you think of our island so far," he was asked by his cousin. "It is beautiful. I am so happy to be here. My parents spoke often about Cyprus, but I did not realize such beauty because I had not seen it with my own eyes."

"Peter, do you know who I am?" "No, I do not know." "I am Maria, your first cousin. My mother is the sister of your father. Here you will meet many more cousins from both sides of your family." "I am so pleased to have so many members of my family here. I thought there was no one left on the island. No brothers, sisters, nor cousins. I am indeed thrilled to be near all of you."

Maria is Mr. Aristides favorite niece. From a child she stood out for her kindness and deep understanding of the needs of others. It was to Maria that Mr. Aristides made the request to find an appropriate bride for his son, and indeed she did.

The parents of Helen (the young lady that has been chosen/matched for Peter) invited to their home the family from America and their relatives in Cyprus. Peter is so impressed by the beauty of this island since his arrival. Now he understands the love his parents have for their homeland. It is not only its natural beauty that attracts him but also its people. These people are different. They are simple people that are warm, friendly, and inviting. You are treated as part of the family even if you were a stranger.

The girl's family of the young prospective bride gave that island welcome to Peter, his parents, and his entire family. The families knew the plan to introduce these two young people to each other, but the prospective bride and groom were unaware. Yet when their eyes met for the first time, love emerged. It was indeed love at first sight and their conspirators were happy. They were satisfied that their secret plan will proceed without obstacles.

That evening in the house of Mr. Aristides' niece who hosted the parents and their son, the discussion was lively. They talked about their visit to the Helen's house and the kind and welcoming treatment they received there. Peter was happy. He could not hide his happiness. He talked with his mother prior to seeking sleep. "Mama, what is it that I am feeling. I liked that young lady very much. Please do not tell my father. I do not wish for him to get upset with me."

"My child, I too liked that young lady. Do not be concerned. If I liked her, I am sure so did your father. Also, there is the fact that you are now an adult. If you wish to marry her that is your choice, assuming she feels the same. Let us see how it goes." "Mama, are you telling me the truth? Is it my choice if I wish to marry her." "Yes, it is and if you are in love with her, I will help you to marry her."

"Mama, thank you very much. I love you." The son said "goodnight" to his mother and departed for his bedroom on the first floor of the house where the children of his cousin occupied. The mother and father were situated in a second floor bedroom that was prepared for them by their niece. "Aristides, we have succeeded. God has helped us with our plan. Our son is in love with the young woman we have chosen for him."

"How do you know?" "He told me so tonight. He is crazy about her." "Thanks be to God." The parents of the young lady after the departure of their guests proceed to their bedroom and begin to discuss the evening quietly. The husband asks his wife. "My wife, what did your think of the young man?" "My husband, I am very happy. The young man is wonderful. He is handsome, young, and hard working. More importantly our daughter was attracted to him. I saw it in her face and in her eyes."

"Well, then I believe all will be well." The young American did not sleep well that night in his cousin's house. He fell in love at first sight with this wonderful young lady. Her face, her eyes, her lips, images haunted him throughout the night not allowing for sleep. The next day his face showed his exhaustion. "Peter, my son you did not sleep well. I see it in your face."

"Yes, mother, I did not sleep well at all." "Why, my child? Was the bed not comfortable for you?" "No, no not at all, all was well with the bed and the bedroom. The problem is the young girl. I believe, mama, that I am in love with her. What can I now do? How can I approach her and talk with her? And once I do what do I say to her?"

"Okay my son, please settle down. I will take care of everything." The next day the aunt spoke with Maria, Mr. Aristides's niece about the matter. "Maria, I know you must realize that our plans have succeeded. My son fell in love with the girl." "I did realize it my dear aunt, and I am very happy and glad I was able to help implement this plan. The young girl is indeed beautiful and comes from a good family."

"For all your assistance in this matter I thank you, Maria. You did a wonderful thing for these two young people and their families. Her beauty enticed my son. Peter is determined to spend time with the girl. To get to know her, speak with her. Can you make the arrangements for these two young people to meet?"

"Of course I can, my aunt." "Thank you, my child." Maria called Helen's mother to tell her that the young man wishes to date her daughter. The mother happily accepted because she knew that her daughter would want this. "Maria, tell Mr. Peter that he is welcome to come to our home, and in the evening he can go out with Helen." The cousin speaks with her cousin.

"Peter, the mother of the young girl has invited you to her home in the evening so that you and Helen can go out on a date. Do you agree?" "Maria, absolutely I wish to do so. I will go to her home. I am very grateful for your help." Peter rented a car and put on his best clothes and bought a bouquet of red carnations. When evening came, he knocked on Helen's door. The mother opened the door politely and with much joy. She welcomed the young visitor.

"Welcome, Mr. Peter, please come in." "Thank you and a few flowers for you." "What beautiful flowers, thank you." Helen is standing next to her mother and her face lights up as she sees Peter. She takes the bouquet from her mother's arms and places the flowers in a decorative vase. The power of love leaves their eyes and bodies and moves into the hearts of these two young people for a second time. The submission brought on by love is evident in both.

The two young people and the mother are now sitting on the sofa and chairs in the living room. The girl is now shaking with the fear of the unknown. Peter and Helen are now ready to leave the comfort of her home to venture outside on their first date. Anticipation and fear as to what is to come takes hold of both of them. Beyond the door waits the rented car, an American car for the pair to enter. The mother with tears of happiness in her eyes closes the door behind them. The phone rings and it is Maria, Peter's cousin, on the other end of the line.

"Mrs. Haroula, how is everything going? Is Peter still there?" "They just left. They are going for a walk together. They seem so happy, Maria. It is obvious that they like each other." "I do know. My cousin cannot hide his feeling. He is definitely in love with Helen." "And Helen feels the same way towards him. She told me. She liked Peter very much." "Good, Mrs. Haroula. We will wait and see how it all develops." "Always know Maria that I will never forget the good thing you have done for us."

Peter's parents know that their son has gone to meet with the girl. They heard the exchange between their niece and the mother of the girl. They heard about their walk, their date. They are thrilled that their plan worked. They are happy. They just have to wait for the final execution of their plan.

The car with the lovers is on its way to the island's capital, Nicosia. It is not far from the village where they are living. Peter is driving. Helen is next to him with her eyes fixed on his face. She cannot get enough of him. She admires him. Her heart is pounding in her chest but beating just for him. Peter with his eyes fixed one eye on the road and the other eye on the angel sitting next to him. The angel he fell in love with at first sight.

"Peter where are we going? May I call you by your first name? I feel like I have known you for many years." "Helen, may I also call you by your first name? I too feel like I have known you for a very long time, maybe since birth. We have known each other well before we were introduced."

Peter extended his right hand and wrapped it around Helen's waist. Helen in turn wrapped both her arms around Peter's waist. Their heads came close, their lips parted, and their first true kiss sealed their love. "You asked me where we are going. We are going to Nicosia. I have been told that it is not far from here."

"Why did you not tell me? I had no idea where we were going. It is so beautiful there. It is a large city which I know well. I went to high school there and would often return to the village by bus. It is only twelve kilometers from the village. My father goes into the city every morning for his work."

"I did not wish to tell you where we were going because I wanted to surprise you. I had reserved a special table in a particular restaurant so we could get acquainted. But I was wrong. I did not realize that we had known each other already since birth. I did not know much about your beautiful island, but it is not difficult to learn about it if one chooses to do so. That is how I figured out where we are going. I love it here especially when I am accompanied by an angel such as you."

Helen was touched by Peter's words and hugged him more intently. As they arrive at the restaurant the young man in love took his beloved's hand and together, they walked into the restaurant. A wonderful place in a perfect world. The maître d' led them to their special table. They were truly in love. With their love filled eyes they saw only each other. The world around them had disappeared. They felt an inexplicable attraction to each other and could not resist. "Helen, I love you," "I too love you, Peter." "Do you wish to be married, my love? Do you wish to return with me to America?"

"Yes, I do Peter. I will go with you to America or anywhere else you choose. I just want to be with you." "You have made me very happy." "I am very happy, too." They ate and drank with much enjoyment in each other's company. They finished their dinner and left the restaurant to a perfectly beautiful warm night. They walked together in each other's arms unaware of the passing of time. It was very late when they decided to return home.

Their love was further sealed with a second intense kiss. It was 1:00 A.M. when Peter returned to his temporary home and his mother, as always, was waiting up for him. She could not sleep for she was anxious to know the outcome. Did they decide as a couple to go forward together? As soon as she opened the door, she had her answer in her son's face. She understood and hugged her son knowing that all was to be what she had hoped for.

"Mama, I am so very happy and lucky. Helen and I are in love, and we wish to be married. But I am afraid that my father will create problems for me and insist that I am still too young to be married."

"No my child. Your father and I would like you to marry. You are now grownup, and we respect your decisions. Before you were very young, and it was appropriate for your father to intervene but not now. He will be happy to hear you are in love and wish to marry this young lady." "Oh, mama you are indeed my angel and always will be. I love you very much, very much."

The son said "goodnight" to his mother and went to bed. He lay on his bed unable to sleep, restless, and he could not close his eyes. A picture of his beloved emerged clearly in his mind. Eventually this beautiful image brought him the peace of sleep.

Dawn rises and the bright sun begins its journey across the sky. The parents awaken, Maria is preparing breakfast. Peter is still asleep. Mrs. Hariklia was worried about her son and went to his room to check on him. She approached his bed quietly and saw his content face. She understood that her son was having sweet dreams. She did not wake him but instead closed the door quietly and left his room. The parents went out onto the patio. Their niece had made up the table outside in the clean air. Their niece's husband joined them and the four individuals enjoyed their coffee and quiet conversation.

"Maria, I believe it is time for us to do something." "What is it we should do, aunt?"

"We should meet with the young girl's parents to discuss the marriage of our children. I believe we are all ready for this outcome." "Yes, aunt, all appears to be ready."

"Maria, I will ask that you notify them, preferably today, I would like the wedding to take place soon before we leave the island" added Mr. Aristides with unbridled enthusiasm and a glow of happiness in his face. The next day Maria called the parents of the future bride. She told them that her aunt and uncle wish to meet with them to discuss their children. The parents answered and invited them to their home that very evening while their two children would be away. The future mother in law was sure that the two love birds would spend time together away from home this evening as they have done so every night.

Peter is ready and eager to meet with his beloved. He goes to her house close to sunset. Helen is ready and waiting at the door and they depart for the road following the sun as it begins its descent with red brilliance into the sea.

It is now much later close to 8 P.M., Mr. Aristides and Mrs. Hariklia and their niece and her husband knock on the door of their future in laws. They spoke with each other at length and decided because their stay is short that the wedding must happen soon. Yet before they proceed with their plans, they felt it was important to speak individually with their children to confirm their agreement. The next day the father spoke with his son.

"Peter, do you love and wish to marry this young lady?" "Yes, father. I love her and wish to marry her." "Helen," asks the father of the young lady, "do you love the young man and wish to marry him." "Yes, father, I do love him and wish to marry him."

June is finished and July provides warmth and beauty. One month is gone yet the Americans are still on the island. Peter forgot about his agreement with his parents that they were to remain in Cyprus for only one month. He did not realize how quickly the days passed. He had forgotten about his plans and his restaurant. He had forgotten his homeland and wished to stay on the island.

The wedding was to take place the penultimate Sunday of the month of July. Happy are the parents of the groom and happy are the parents of the bride. The two lovebirds are now to be united in the bonds of matrimony. Mr. Aristides. Mrs. Hariklia, and their niece are grateful. Their plan came to furnishment well beyond their expectations. The day of their wedding approaches.

The bride and groom are getting ready as the day, the selected Sunday all anxiously waiting for, has arrived. Wedding guests begin to enter the vestibule of the Church. Peter is standing next to his father, his sponsor, his best man, and his friends, holding a bouquet of white roses as he awaits his beloved.

The limousine, adorned with white ribbons and flowers, did not take long to appear. The door opened and, in its opening, the beautiful Helen of Troy was seen, wife to be with her white wedding dress and the crown/veil on her head. She climbs up the steps of the church leading to the large courtyard holding on to her father. On the other side of the courtyard are waiting, the Bishop who is ready to marry and bless the couple, the groom with nervousness as his heart beats faster as this beauty approaches, his father, the sponsor, and the cantors. The bride's parents deliver their daughter to the man who will be the future partner for their child.

The courtyard is large, but the church is small. There are many attendees, so the wedding is done outside in the fresh air. The Bishop has his holy books in hand and the couple is now in front of him and so the wedding begins. The first part of the ceremony is the Ceremony of the Betrothal. The rings are given by the sponsor and exchanged on the fingers of the couple three times and a blessing is given. The Ceremony of the Marriage then begins.

The Bishop concludes with the words, "Who God has joined together, let no one put asunder." The sponsor, which is their niece Maria, exchanges their white crowns joined by a single white ribbon three times representing their union with a common bond. Following the final blessing, the priest takes the hands of the couple and leads them around the altar three times. The symbolism here is to have God, their faith, be with them together as they go through life. The couples hands are joined together, and the Bishop's hands surrounds their hands as he leads them.

The ceremony has ended, and the air is filled with rice and beautifully colored almonds falling like hail onto the heads of the beloved couple. Handshakes, blessings, hugs, and kisses for the newly married couple from their family, friends, and fellow villagers. The limousine is waiting on the road. It took the two lovebirds away and would return them later for their reception in a beautiful hall in Nicosia.

The Cypriot dances, songs and much joy continued into the early hours of the next day. The light of the dawn illuminated the faces of the happy people in attendance. The celebration finished and the attendees returned to their homes. The young couple flew out that night to Athens for their honeymoon. The parents of the couple remained behind. After one month's time the newly married couple returned to an apartment in Nicosia for the length of time they are to remain in Cyprus.

The father came to visit his son. "Peter, now you must begin the process of preparing the paperwork required by the US Immigration Department so that Helen can legally enter the US as your spouse. Your mother and I must leave soon. I will take care of the restaurant until your return. I am feeling well, my health is wonderful."

"Okay, father, I will do as you say. It is not appropriate that I leave now without Helen. I must stay and wait until her visa is finished and we will come back home together." After one week Peter's parents left for their return home to America. Their joy endless and their luck great. They had managed to marry their son with a young lady from their homeland. Their perfect and beautiful dream was achieved with incredible success. Mr. Aristides can now die grateful to God and to his fate.

He returned to the restaurant the following day. John his trusted employee took good care of everything. The restaurant ran as clockwork not showing any deficiencies because of the absence of father and son. Mr. Aristides does not feel any tiredness at all as he visits the restaurant daily to prepare it for the return of his son. His health is wonderful. The result of his efforts to protect his son's future added an additional thirty years to his life.

Three months passed and the visa was finally done to open the door to a new world for Helen. She was prepared to enter this door. The happy couple say goodbye to Helen's parents, relatives on both sides with many hugs and kisses and promises that they will call/write often. Hugging each other they take their seats on the plane arriving the same day to the land of Christopher Columbus that awaits them.

The overjoyed father, in the meantime as he waits for the children to return, has rented and furnished a beautiful apartment close to his home in the same neighborhood for the young couple. The young wife overwhelmed by this new world is consoled in the arms of her new loving parents. Spending her days with them allows her not to miss the family she left behind and her beloved island. She is deeply in love with her husband and is happy to be with him in her new home which they share. She is even more happy about something else that she shares with her husband.

"Peter. I believe that I am pregnant." "Helen, what are you saying. Do you believe you are pregnant?" "Yes, Peter." "Tomorrow we will visit with the doctor to confirm." The next day they went to see their doctor. It was confirmed that she was indeed pregnant. "Young man, your wife is at six weeks." Much happiness for the new couple. The young couple quickly became a family. Mr. Aristides became a grandfather. He could not believe his ears.

"Father, are you happy? If it is a boy, he will have your name. If it is a girl, she will have my mother's name." The young husband and father was to be recalled to his job he enjoyed which he had forgotten during his time in the arms of his love on the island of Aphrodite. Now he is stronger and more willing to take the road to return to his work which he had left behind. He loves his father and cares for him.

At home he has his father living with him in the care of his mother and his wife. A new daughter has joined his family. This wonderful father has not only one son but a daughter and thrills to be with them. The younger man's family is everything to him but it is work and the plans he has made for the restaurant that keep him up at night. His wife lies next to him, yet he thinks of his restaurant. His business is now his priority.

His wife has become less important than the attainment of success as a businessman. The woman whom with her love made him forget everything now knows she cannot win him back. She feels alone in a country that is not hers. She is amongst people that love her, but it is not her parents. She begins to close herself off from all those around feeling nothing but loneliness, her only companion. She is convinced that the man that loved her deeply on her island no longer loves her. His choice now is to give his love elsewhere.

Mr. Aristides and his wife love their son's bride as their own child. They spend days and nights with her, trying to comfort her, but with no avail. Their son is never home, busy all day and all night. They barely see him, and he barely spends time with them. He leaves the house at early dawn only to return home after midnight.

There is a toll on his entire family. His father is happy for his son's success yet on occasion feels an unusual pain in his chest. He finally decides to see his doctor. His examination shows mixed results, so more drugs are prescribed. Many more recommendations from his physician. Mr. Aristides is upset with his current health situation that does not allow him to work as before. To help his son and to lighten his load.

He cannot deal with his condition. Yet although his condition worries him it is not as important to him as his son's attitude towards his wife. His son's indifference towards his wife concerns him greatly. He sees the sadness in the eyes of his new daughter, and it hurts him deeply.

Both parents try to tell their son about his behavior and how it is affecting his wife but to no avail. The son chooses not to change his behavior. The parents are worried but mostly the father. The excitement of being a grandfather is overshadowed by the problems in his son's marriage. Mr. Aristides felt that he had chosen unwisely for his son. He could see his son's indifference in his face, he could not bear it.

Two months later Mr. Aristides was taken by ambulance in the middle of the night to the emergency room of the hospital, his heart had stopped. The good father that did not get the chance to meet his first grandson, was now gone. It was a shock for the son. He never expected to lose his father. His attachment to his father was his awakening. His unconditional love for him awaken the lover to the reality that his devotion to his work which he inherited from his father needed to change.

His father's death changed something inside of him. Something he had not understood until then, that apart from the dedication he had to his career, there were people around him who loved him and needed him. The young man woke up and looked around him. He saw his mother, his wife, but he did not see his father. His father died with sadness in his heart and assumed his son was indifferent towards his wife because she made him unhappy.

He realized that his son did not love the woman he married. He felt that his children were not happy. And that was to end him. It took a long time, many months, for his son to finally accept the loss of his father, to accept that he was no longer with him and part of his life. His mother and his wife are now his family. He is responsible for their happiness as well as the happiness of an unknown face yet to come, and he must put forth all his effort to achieve this. He did not need to wait long to meet this unknown person.

A new life was born, and it was a boy. A son who came to fill the empty place in this family and in the son's life. And so he was given the name of his grandfather, Aristides. The young Aristides will resurrect the memory of his grandfather that is now passed. The pain of loss melted away as snow does under the brilliance and warmth of the sun as it brightens the earth and all its beings.

Slowly some things have been forgotten and other things reemerge in the thoughts of the son now that he has a son. He has remembered the need to work and this time more so for the need to work more was being asked of him for he has more responsibilities. His family is getting larger and so his work once again is taking priority. He returns to his old habits, he leaves at dawn and returns after midnight. He does not have time to spend with his wife nor to play with his newborn. The child is asleep when he leaves and asleep when he returns.

Mrs. Hariklia has a son, a daughter in law, and a grandson. She loves her daughter in law very much for she is very kind and the daughter she has never had. She has forgotten her companion who is now gone. She now hugs her grandson that has taken his place in her thoughts and in her heart.

Helen loves her mother in law very much for she is her second mother. They continue life together. Her mother in law is saddened by the behavior of her son towards his wife and newborn son. She feels her new daughter's grief. Helen loves her husband very much. He too loved her very much in the beginning. What has made his love change? All these thoughts and doubts in her mind. She could not understand his sudden change in his love for her, so her mind began to drift to a dark place, jealousy.

What was wrong with her husband? Why the change in him once we came to this new country? Why was Peter different, so crazy in love with me when we were on my island? Why is he different and does not watch over me as he did before? Questions which have no answers. They fill her mind and sabotaged her thoughts. Thoughts of the reasons for her husband's behavior have become part of her daily reflections. Such thoughts are becoming destructive to their marital relationship.

Helen did not believe that this disease of depression would infect her. It is too late for reprieve and therapy. There is no pharmacological treatment that she could turn to. The pain has become too great, and her soul suffers. Life has lost its joy. She now lives under a constant grey cloud with no sun in sight. The sun cannot warm her cold and diseased heart.

Peter does not understand what is happening around him. The depression he sees in his wife does not make sense. He loves her as always. Nothing has changed. He does not see nor understand the change in her. So he returns to work hoping that all will pass with time. All his attention, energy, focused on his business. Yet, each time he returned home he would see her stoic face and be surprised. He is bothered by her doubt filled investigative eyes. It is almost as if she is judging him and determining if she likes the man she married.

CHAPTER THREE: PETER BECOMES A BUSINESS SUCCESS

After the death of the Peter's father he emersed himself whole heartedly into his establishment. He wants his business to grow and be more successful than all the other neighboring and even beyond restaurants. Even beyond the restaurants located in Manhattan. He wanted his restaurant to become known for elegant dining and to attract the rich and famous. It is to be well-recognized and famous throughout the world. His trusted employee and that of his father, Mr. John, has been helping him to obtain such a vision with his own many years of experience.

"Peter I would like to share a suggestion with you now that you are the owner. I once made this proposal to your father, but he was not interested in pursuing it. I believe you will be more open to my proposal because you have more modern ideas and highly technological ideas." "What is your proposal, Mr. John?" "Listen, in order for the restaurant to progress and evolve, as you have dreamed of it, some things will need to change. Our current space is large, but the space is not used well. We need to make renovations to create a more elegant atmosphere. Do you want that? Also, we need to address our staffing policy. Currently we have two waiters, both men. They have worked here for a long time. We do not have women working as waitresses. We need both men and women. We also need young as well as older staff. Diversity in our staff will bring in customers. Your father would not make such changes in staff. What do you think?"

"What can I say, I have not thought about it. Do what you think best because you have the knowledge and experience. All I have is only the dream." Mr. John proceeded to implement his plan as per the support of his new young owner. He completed all the renovations. He implemented the staff changes. He decided to keep the two older men in the older section of the restaurant and hired three women for the newer more modern addition. He was gifted in promotion, and he publicized the new restaurant bringing in many new patrons.

Three beautiful and hard working waitresses brought in a younger male crowd. Each one was more beautiful than the last. The youngest amongst them touched the heart and soul within Peter. Her blue eyes and blonde hair reminded him of a long ago love, now lost. He felt enslaved once again by this young woman. So again he has forgotten his family, his mother, wife, and child. He leaves early every morning just to be close to this new employee.

Happy indeed is Peter but he must keep his feelings and attraction for this angel, hidden. She must live only in his dreams and never emerge into the light of day. She is his employee, and he is her employer. He must respect her position as well as his own. He cannot take advantage of his position as her boss. Also, he is not free to pursue such a relationship. He is married with a wife and a child and of course he must consider the difference in age. All these thoughts prayed on his mind and kept him at an appropriate stance and distance from the young lady.

The three new waitresses are called Anna, Maria, and Alkmini and they beautify the new establishment. Their presence adds to his profits and indeed fills his tables. Mr. John was so right, thought Peter, that for so many years as he continued to push us to implement his plan. My father declined to pursue such a plan. I am sure he had his reasons. I gave the green light to implement all.

The mother and wife would often visit the restaurant. The mother was indifferent, but the wife was vigilant. She just could not understand and did not wish to accept the change in her beloved companion. Her suspicions arose in her mind clouding her beautiful face and jealousy began to burn in her soul. His focus was the success of his business and another matter that brought him up at dawn to the Bronx and returned him home to Astoria after midnight. He has no time for his mother, his wife, and his child.

His mother now not unlike his father in the past, close to the bride feels her pain, her loneliness. The mother is now alone in her efforts as she tries to address this issue with her son. He is indifferent and unaware as to what is happening around him. He is convinced that it is not his fault. He truly does not know what he could have done to have created this situation. He loves his family, his mother, his wife, and his child. Yet this love is in theory only, not in practice, and even that love is starting to fade.

He is in love with his young waitress. He cannot breath without her presence, for she is his source of oxygen. In the evening with many excuses he convinces her to stay after all the employees have left for the day. He drives her home every night to Flushing where she lives such as a father would do for his young daughter to protect her from the dangers of the night. This daily trip makes him happy.

Alkmini respects her employer as she would her father. She sees his actions as being those of a work family, no different than her own family. Her employer is a trusted member of this family as is her father a trusted member of the other family. She feels happy and blessed to have both.

This constant daily attention grows day to day. What was once respect for her employer grew into admiration and ultimately to love. But not the love a daughter would feel for her father, but as a love of a wife for her husband.

The young employee loved her employer. She loves him just as intensely as he loves her. Her eyes show her love for him. Their eyes are mirrors of their mutual attraction and love, yet their actions try to contradict their mutual desire for each other. She feels special and attractive to have such a man touch her heart and fill it with the sweet music of love. She feels worshiped and loved. Young Aristides has turned one year's old. Mother and grandmother are preparing for his birthday at their home. Friends and family are invited for a Sunday event. Most people do not work on that day, but her husband does work. He does not take a single day off per week, per month, per year. He does not remember memorable dates such as birthdays. Very tired he returns home every evening late. His mind is elsewhere most of the time, in the clouds.

"Peter, do you know what event is on this coming Sunday?" asks the forlorn wife. "No, I do not know." "Well, where do you live. Have you lost your mind. I know you have forgotten me, but have you forgotten your child, too?" "What is wrong with the child?" "Do you not remember the date of his birth?" "Oh, yes, Sunday is his birthday. Time does indeed fly!!" "Okay, so maybe on that day you will remain home as all good families do, to spend time with their wives and children." "You are making this very difficult for me. You know that the restaurant must be open every day of the week and cannot close its doors."

"I know that your restaurant is the exception. All others have at least one day when they are closed. You choose not to be apart from your restaurant. You also have Mr. John that can manage the restaurant for you while you are away. It depends on you unless of course you have another reason why you cannot stay away from the restaurant."

Peter realized where this conversation was going and chose not to continue. "Helen, I am very tired, and we still have time to discuss this further before Sunday." "Just for your information we will have many people attending, mostly our old friends. Do you remember them. I invited them." "Absolutely, I remember them. I am glad you invited them." "That is why it is critical that you be here." "Okay, I will be there."

"Did you not invite any of your employees?" she asked with a suspicious and sarcastic voice. Peter understood who she was talking about. He looked at his wife's eyes and gave her an indignant look. He threw his jacket onto the chair and opened up the bedroom door. "I told you that I am tired, and I wish to sleep. I am not in the mood for conversation." "Okay, do not get angry. I just asked one question. If you wish to invite anyone of your employees." "I do not know, maybe."

It was way past midnight. Peter's fatigue and irritability overwhelmed his nerves. It was too late for him to fall asleep. Annoyed by her suspicions that were driving her she waited for her husband to fall asleep and laid down next to him with her eyes open. She stared at the ceiling fantasizing of her husband in the arms of an unknown other. The poison of her suspicions fueled her jealousy and allowed it to grow day after day darkening her soul.

The week progresses and Sunday is coming soon. Peter's constant thoughts evolve around his young love, his employee, Alkmini. She is the only employee that has off on Sundays. The other employees have days scattered throughout the week. I will invite her to my son's birthday and that will be my final decision.

"Alkmini, do you have plans for this coming Sunday? Are you free?" "Yes, Mr. Peter, I am free. I have potential plans to go with a girlfriend to the movies on Sunday, but I can postpone my plans if you wish me to do so. Is it important that I come to the restaurant?"

"No, forget about work, I would like you to come somewhere else. On Sunday we will have the first birthday celebration for my son. I was hoping to invite you to this event, of course, if you wish to come. What do you say?" "Mr. Peter, I would love with all my heart to be part of such a joyous event for your family." "Thank you for thinking of me," answered the lovesick employee to her employer. "Good, I will pick you up from your home and bring you to mine."

Peter's wife was happy that he would stay home and would be part of the celebration for the birthday of their child. This was her first victory with her husband. It is early Sunday morning, and she works with her mother in law to make all the preparations. They decorate the house, prepare the food and the table, bake the cake, and add the multicolored candles to be blown when the time comes by the young child.

"Helen, I have to leave but will return shortly." "Where are you going? In two hours all will arrive, and we must be ready." "I will be quick and arrive back on time." "Okay, go," said the wife with closed tense lips. The time has arrived, and friends/family are at the door. A few minutes later Peter's car pulls into the driveway, and he opens his car door. In the front passenger seat next to the driver, sits a young and beautiful girl. Most of his friends recognized her as the young waitress at the restaurant.

Peter's wife and guardian of her family did not expect such a surprise from her much loved husband. Her face clearly showed her annoyance. She did not speak; she did not express her feelings. She was gracious and invited the young girl into her home as she did with all her guests. Yet she knew that her husband was treading a very dangerous road of no return.

The celebration is over, and everyone has gone. The lovesick man returns his employee to her home. The wife locks herself in her boudoir. The mother in law understood all! She notices that the sky is accumulating black clouds. She feels a torrential rain is coming. She is afraid that this loving couple will not be able to survive the flood that awaits them. They have lost their protective umbrella, mutual trust, and respect.

Peter returns happy and cheerful. All the lights are off in the house, electricity was lost. The welcome was dark and cold. The warmth of his home was gone. "Helen, I am happy that the birthday event for our son was so beautiful." "Is it the beauty of the event that has made you so happy or is it the beauty of the one you brought to our celebration? You must realize that her beauty is in your eyes only."

"Did you not tell me to invite someone from work?" "I did not ask you to invite someone. I asked you if you intended to invite someone." "I answered you, maybe, it depends." "And you invited the only one that matters to you, because you cannot breathe unless she is beside you. Is she the only employee? Are there no others?"

"I invited her because she is the only one that has off on Sundays. The others have different days off during the week. Today is Sunday. Why is this a problem? Why are you upset? I truly do not understand, and I am afraid because I do not know where you are going with this." "It is good that you are afraid." The sky on Sunday afternoon suddenly turned cloudy and dark and by nightfall of the same day all the clouds completely blanketed the sky and turned all totally dark. All night long there was a torrential rain and there was no indication that this dark rain would stop in the coming days.

Helen could no longer deal with this situation, as she thought she could. Yesterday she thought she was victorious in that she convinced her husband to take a day off and celebrate with his family their child's birthday. The result was the opposite of a victory. At the end 'it was a loss'. She now needed to gather up all her strength, her courage and to make a stand. She had no other choice.

"Do you love your wife? Do you wish us to continue to live together? Do you wish to continue as a family whose foundation was born in love? You once offered me very much love, but today you offer this love to someone else." "Of course I wish us to stay together. I want this because the love I offered you once is the same today. It has not changed."

"It did not change. Is that what you think? So where is your great love you once had for me that brought us together on the island? Why did it disappear when I came to this unknown land for me and known to you? I was expecting you would take my hand and give me the courage I needed for us to go forward together in life in your country. You forgot me very quickly. Other things, other people were more important to you, and you focused all your energy and time on these things. It is not too late for you to open your eyes and to see the correct path you must take. The road you are now following is rough with downward steep slopes and sudden cliffs."

"What do you mean?" "I mean that when someone decides to live their life with someone else, they are no longer alone, just one person. They have a responsibility in a relationship to consider the needs and desires of the other person as they do for themselves. It is a union and as a union it must direct its actions collectively. You can do it if you want to. I emphasize this. "If you want." I am asking you to dedicate two days starting now, each week, to spend with your family. It depends on you. They will change many unpleasant things that poison our lives currently."

"Is that your problem? That I do not spend more time with my family? Then let me know how to satisfy your needs. I have told you many times that what I do and do not do, I do out of ambition to create a company better than others. I made it better. At least I think so. And that is why I am not intimately involved in our daily dealings. But I will think about your proposal, and I believe I can do something to address your needs."

"I cannot wait! Your family and your child, whom I believe you love, are waiting for you." "Do you want or need anything else?" "No, not at the moment." This "not at the moment" statement from his wife played in Peter's mind. He felt that the current somewhat peaceful antagonism that is only at the beginning stage can have devastating consequences as it becomes more aggressive.

Helen applauds her second attempt and hopes that the future victory will not be lost, like the previous one. That is why she is watching and waiting patiently to see if indeed he finds a way to satisfy her request. The occupation of the territory to be conquered piece by piece, without the fear of losing the whole. Peter decides to find a way to satisfy Helen's request and desires, thinking that this way he would be able to avoid any future actions and attacks she might be planning for him. He spoke with his experienced director, Mr. John.

"Mr. John, I believe we have established a successful business over the many years together. Now it is the time for us to obtain some rest for ourselves and to spend time with our families." "What do you mean, Mr. Peter."

"I am thinking of giving our employees two days off and not just one that they currently have with no decrease in salary. We will also give ourselves two days off as well. Currently we do not even take one day off, you and me. We have forgotten that we have families. What do you think about this?" "Whatever you want, Mr. Peter. I do not have any objections." "Then proceed to work on it. You have the authority."

By the following month all was in place as per the wish of the annoyed wife, who had more surprises for her unsuspecting husband. Mr. John arranged the employees five day week schedule. Priority was given to the boss to allow him time off over the two weekend days. All other schedules were staggered to insure continuous coverage for each day uninterrupted. Mr. John gave himself Monday/Tuesday off. He even gave the young employee the same schedule as her employer for Mr. John understood his boss' weakness.

Peter's wife was very happy with the outcome for it was what she desired. Her husband is with her two days a week. The father can spend time with his son two days a week. Yet in the face of her partner she sees the unhappiness of a man stripped of his freedom and imprisoned. It wounds her to know that he does not wish to spend time with her and his child. It is difficult for now and she must be patient. Only time will bring him back. She will win back a man she loves so much. She will work on clearing all obstacles that exist between them and is determined to turn back time to their first meeting and happy union.

Mrs. Hariklia is very happy with her son's decision to remember that besides work there is his family. She does not know what her daughter in law is thinking, nor does she care. She is not concerned with her exploits. She is only concerned about her son. She just wants him to be happy. Something many mothers want for their child. She wishes that her two children, groom and bride recover the happiness and love they once had for each other. Also, she wishes to see from this happiness emerge her future grandchildren. She hopes that the roof they initially created over them keeps them now protected from the cold in the winter and the heat in the summer.

"My child, I am so very happy that you have finally found some time to spend with us. You do know that your son until today does not know you. You are a stranger to him. When you leave in the morning, he is asleep. When you return at night, he is asleep. He never sees you. See now as you hold him in your arms how he is staring at you. He is trying to recognize you. He knows me and his mother because he sees us all day and all night. You he does not know because he has never seen you. Please stay with us from this day on so he can get to know you too. If you chose to do so you will be rewarded with a blessed life and your family will survive and flourish."

"You are so very right, mama. I understand it and I acknowledge it. My mistake of the past was indeed tremendous. I was so very obsessed with obtaining success at all costs. I can now feel the change in me. Holding my son in my arms and his embrace warms my heart. The embrace of a woman brought this realization to me. The embrace of a woman that loves me very much and wishes that I am always besides her. I am happy that I can be with all of you even if it is for a little while." "Thank you, my child."

The weekend has come to an end. Monday has emerged. His arms once again will embrace but this time it will be someone different. His eyes, mind and heart will embrace the angel that pulls him out of the darkness of the weekend and into the light of day. Yet this limited light shines only in a small corner that barely can be seen or warmed by this hidden love. Peter is anxious to have left his home. He is no different from a convict who is given the opportunity to leave his prison. He is free and can be with his heart's desire. He cannot hide his happiness as it is reflected in the mirror. His happiness is there for his wife as well. Together they shared breakfast, kiss each other goodbye and separate until they meet again late at night

The husband's secret love, Alkmini, will begin her shift at eleven o'clock in the morning until seven o'clock in the evening. She works the evening shift. The wish of her boss is to be able to accompany her to her home on those winter nights. All employees, morning or evening, work for eight hours, with the exception of the boss and his manager, who start first and end last thereby completing twelve hours.

As the day emerges into almost midday, the employer's face begins to light up because he sees the face of his young employee. The long absence of his love over the weekend will soon be over. Her reappearance brings back his distant heart that had been tucked away. The tedious workday is now over, and the working staff leaves the place of work. Mr. John is the last to leave, and he locks the doors.

The charming employee waits for her employer to accompany her, as usual. In the car the driver sits and next to him his love. This secret love that does not allow itself to be seen in the light of day, afraid of shining. A strong glow that blinds all who see it. He is protected by the dark. The middle aged employer and his employee in her youth are now traveling on a long road with many obstacles as this illegitimate relationship begins.

Reason loses to emotions, and love becomes affection. It appears on the surface to be a father-daughter relationship with the duty of a father to accompany his daughter to her house. For the man, a kiss and caress of the young hand completes his dream and begins the rejuvenation of a middle-aged man's heart. The young woman feels her heart to begin to grow. The distance that had separated them in the past is now gone. These two hearts are now united in a single happy beat.

Peter leaves his love at her home in Flushing. Happiness carries him to his next stop, his house in Astoria. His wife is waiting for him. The obvious joy in the face of her husband brings her joy too. She understands him. She wants him happy. She is happy to have him near her now. Even for only a short time. She will win him over completely later, for the fight continues.

Helen is expecting their second child. Peter is happy at the prospect of being a father. Mrs. Hariklia regained her happiness of the family once again. Husband, wife, and mother-in-law, all are in total temporary happiness. Temporary happiness, because there is no guarantee as to whether it will take root in the right soil or not. The growth of the tree depends on the food and water that it needs and on those willing to take care of it, those who love it. Those that need it to exist in order to protect them with its shade during the hot days of the heat.

The month is May and Astoria full of sun and light. Colorful flowers emerge in yards, gardens, and parks. It is Saturday and all members of the family are together. The two-day compulsory concession has been agreed upon and upheld. The couple accompany their baby to Astoria Park and sit under the big tree. The same outing took place forty years ago by another set of parents and another baby. Helen is wondering if the time is right to make the request that has long been haunting her brain. She wonders how her husband will take her request and if he will accept it. "Peter, if I ask you a favor, will you do it for me?" "What is the favor? (The husband's voice was cut off from fear and anxiety). What is this favor that you are asking for?"

"Peter, do you remember when we got married and left Cyprus? Since we came here, you and I have not returned to my island. It has been quite a few years. I have longed to see my parents and my brother again. Would you want to go there again with me? Will you do this for me, which I really need right now?" Peter breathed easily and the anxiety dissipated. The favor request was different from what he expected. It has nothing to do with his own schedule or behavior. His unique love relationship was safe for now. He will not allow anyone to take it away, he will not lose it. "Helen, you are right. I had not thought of that. Forgive me for being so short-sighted and selfish. Let us go together to see your family this summer if you agree."

The husband is in a hurry to satisfy his wife's wish, which will definitely be to his advantage, because his consent will stop any other unwanted desires of hers. "Thank you, my love." Helen also felt that she had won the second battle. The plan proceeded carefully along the lines drawn to win the war and with it the gain, to date, of the lost ground.

Summer has arrived. The preparations are all done. Peter spoke to his manager, Mr. John, to continue the efficient operation of his restaurant on his own until Peter returns from his trip. A month away would not be too difficult, he thought. Will it work? Will I be able to tolerate it, Maybe, I can. I must try.

Peter, Helen, and the young Aristides are off to Kennedy Airport for their trip to Cyprus. Helen is so pleased and happy that she hugs her husband frequently. She is looking forward to seeing her homeland and family once again. The plane begins its ascent into the cloud filled sky that overlooks this big metropolis of the world. In about nine hours this sky will blend into another sky, a blue sky overlooking the beauty of their new destination. The family finally set foot on the island's soil after many days. Helen opened both doors and windows to let the familiar wind of her place cool her lungs and then closed them in order to hug her family who were waiting for her with love and anticipation.

Helen has one brother, younger than her, Nikko. He is engaged to be married and the wedding is scheduled to coincide with his older sister's stay on the island. The future new sister is introduced to Helen and Peter. The island of Aphrodite is full of such Aphrodites. Peter, whose journey was compulsory and necessary for him to do, found himself in the place with new memories to replace the past. The recent picture in his mind of his blonde haired blue eyed love now changes.

The blonde angel with the blue eyes shines as part of his past and Aphrodite of Cyprus takes her place with her black hair and black eyes. His brother-in-law's fiancée is very beautiful. The older brother- in-law follows her with his eyes. The wife from America forgot to watch her unfaithful American husband. But she remembered suddenly when her brother introduced them to his fiancée. Her concerned eye caught the well-known stare of her husband aimed on the beauty that was in front of him. Her mind did not want this again. Her fate established in the fool that she married chased her wherever she went.

Throughout the rest of the trip, the couple were not able to speak with each other. A fake smile on her lips. His face is full of clouds. Obvious sadness of absence of love and trust between them. Not many hours passed after arrival, and he was once again immersed in lust for someone else. The gleam in his eyes shone now on the face of a new star in his constantly alternating sky. His wife was once again gone from his world. The wife's sky turned black. The rain from the dark clouds will soon fall and the flood will once again drown Helen. How could he do this to her on her special island and in front of her family?

Helen does not feel well, she is dizzy. A chest pain overwhelms her and makes it difficult to breathe. The poison inside her kills her existence once again. The bitterness pushed away her joy. The joy created by the trip to see its place and its people again.

For a month, the American visitors had arranged to stay in Cyprus. A week has passed since their arrival on the island. Next week will be the wedding of the brother. The decision of the parents, since the sister would be with them during this time. The newlyweds are getting ready. The best man was found — the groom's brother's friend. Peter is happy to spend every day with the brother-in-law. He leaves no opportunity not to see and visit with the future bride. Helen is disappointed with her husband's behavior as he neglects her once again.

By now she knew his tactics when someone young and beautiful came his way. His superficiality has no limits, and it has become unbearable for her, especially here on her island where they first met. Jealousy erupts inside her heart and destroys her soul. She cannot drive away the feeling of inadequacy or being less than she hoped she would be for him. He is enough for her so why can she not be enough for him.

She feels inferior to every beautiful idol that charms the man she loves. She wants him for her own, a unique love just for her. The joy of the journey left her now and only darkness covers her heart. She tries to hide what hurts her, but she cannot. The pain is visible on her face and in her demeanor. Her parents see what is happening to their daughter, especially her mother.

"What is wrong, my child? Your joy was great when you saw us, and we saw you the day before. What has happened to change your mood? Since then something has been tormenting you. I see it in your eyes and in your face. Do you not like it here? What is bothering you, tell me, my child. "

"There is nothing wrong, mother. It is just that pregnancy bothers me. I had the same problem when I was pregnant with my son." "Are you sure about that or is it something else? How are you doing with Peter? Are you happy with him? Does he take good care of you?" "Yes, mother, please let it go!"

Helen was angry at her mother's questions and remarks. She pretended to have some pain and went to lie down. Her husband and her brother went everywhere together. She does not know where he is going although she suspects. A knife opens a new wound to her sick soul. Such unhappiness in a so called love relationship is unbearable for Helen.

The wedding day has arrived on Sunday the second week of July on the beautiful island of Aphrodite. In the church, the groom, his parents, his sister and her husband and many people are waiting for the bride, who finally appears. The doors of the limousine opened, and a beautiful bride appeared. The applause shook the air that smelled of joy and happiness. Helen is standing next to her husband. She is deafened by persistent and incessant applause. The glow in her husband's eyes illuminates his face. A pain in her heart and a dizziness causes her to lose her balance. Peter was surprised and he quickly grabbed her by the armpit to give her support to stand.

The marriage ceremony continues. The crowns are exchanged. And the fiancés are now a formal married couple, according to the rules of the church and the state. This was followed by a reception at the same center where once not that long ago two lovers celebrated their wedding. Happy then but unhappy now. "My love. What does this place remind you of? Do you remember what happened here a few years ago?" Peter whispers in Helen's ears. "Yes. I remember. But you have forgotten." "What are you trying to say?" "Nothing, please leave me alone. I have a headache."

Peter frowned for he could not understand why his wife is behaving so strangely. He does not know what he had done to bring out this aggressive behavior in her once again. He is careful not to go beyond the limits for he would anger her further. Helen's mother does not take her eyes off her daughter's face.

She examines her face and body language throughout the event. She did not believe the excuses given to her by her daughter. Something else is bothering her, she thought. She is sure that something is wrong with her Helen's husband. It is that which is upsetting her beloved daughter.

The celebration is now over, and all the attendees are gone. The honeymooners dipped into their savings and are flying to London, England. Peter's joy flew away with them, and he feels like a stone flattened his chest. The stone is preventing his lungs from functioning and his breathing is heavy. He has not spoken a single word on the way back with his wife and her family to their house.

"What has happened to you, Peter? Where did the joy you have felt the last two weeks go? Why was it lost so suddenly?" "What are you saying again? What joy are you talking about?" "Yes, you know since we came here until today, you have been very happy. You spent time with my brother every day. Now that he is gone, why are you sad? Do you miss him that much?" "Yes, I miss him. If you really want to know why I am now sad well, I am bored here. I want us to leave as soon as possible."

"But you wanted us to come here. Our month stay here is not over as yet." "I do know that the month did not end. The truth is I really like it here. I felt the joy once again; this wonderful place gave us so much happiness not that long ago. But you from the time we came until now, dark clouds have covered your face and your eyes. Nothing seems to make you happy. I do not know what you want from me." "What I wanted, yes and what I want now, is for you to be less stupid. Your inappropriate behavior hides the sun from me and clouds my sky, that once, when I first met you here, was so bright."

Peter did not say a single word in response. He did not understand why his pathological and mentally ill wife said what she said clearly unprovoked. What he wanted now was to go away. Get far away from her and to return to his work. To disappear on that very same night. Speechless and angry, he prepares his suitcase.

"What are you doing there? Where are you going?" "I am going to hell, and if you want, come with me to hell. If you do not want to, stay in your 'so called' paradise." "No, I will join you in the hell that we have created for both of us." The next day the infidel man appeared more upset. They could not hide the angry exchange they had the night before. The mother is anxious for the sight of her daughter in the morning.

"Helen. What is going on? I did not sleep all night listening to the two of you quarrel. Why? Are you having a problem with your husband? What did he do to you?" "Leave me alone, leave me. I have my sorrows and you belittle them with your questions. You are not interested in why I feel this way. Until yesterday, Peter was happy to be here. Today he does not like it and he wants to leave."

"And why should he leave now? Didn't you say you would stay here for a month? There are still two weeks left." "He wants to leave because he lost Nick's company." "Ah but he is correct. They were good friends. He liked him. Now he is alone and has no one to talk to. He has you, that instead of spending time with him and getting closer you have driven him away with your behavior."

"What behavior are you talking about? What do you know about my life?" "I understand somewhat what is happening. Peter is a great man, and he loves you. Watch him and that is all I am saying." "It is best that you do not say anything else. I have heard your advice. I will leave with him. It is not right to let him leave on his own. And do you know why? It is because I love him, and I want to be with him. A simple quarrel does not affect our relationship. If anything it makes it stronger. Our relationship is a difficult one yet a binding one. We cannot live with each other, yet we cannot live apart."

"I understand so try to always stay together and never apart. It depends on you. Do not judge him without proof." Helen understood the insult given by her mother. The phrases "depends on you" and "without reason" reverberated loudly in her mind. Her mother obviously felt that her daughter was jealous of her husband.

"Mama, the phrases "depends on me" and "without reason" let those thoughts be my concern only. You have no reason to concern yourself about it." "All right, my child. I am so sorry." "And I too apologize to you, Mama. Sometimes you make me so angry that I overreact. And again I apologize for behaving so badly. I love you, Mama, you, and all of you, and I am so very sorry that I cannot stay any longer with you, but we have to leave. It is also his job that concerns him. Tonight we will leave."

"My children. It has been so many years without seeing you. We were glad to have you with us. And now you want to depart so quickly. Your father and I will not be able to stay away long from you." "We will be back, Mama, do not worry." "All right, my child. We will be waiting for your return."

With tears in their eyes mother and father embraced their daughter and her husband. The grandmother did not wish to let her grandson leave easily from her arms. She filled her grandson with many kisses on his sweet cheeks. Her first grandchild, who she cared for with immense love and affection for almost three weeks is being taken away so quickly. She was saddened.

Peter is depressed and quiet on the way to the airport. Helen with the child in her arms is obviously distressed. She regretted all that happened and most of all ending their vacation earlier than planned. She had hoped to spend more time on the island she loved and relive those beautiful memories of when they first met.

They sat next to each other on the plane but not a word was exchanged. They both focused on information sheets, magazines in front of them. Helen looks at Peter but does not dare to speak to him. She gets up from her seat to place the child gently in an empty seat next to her instead of her lap. Suddenly a sharp pain in the abdomen causes Helen to grab this area with both hands and fall back into her seat.

"Peter I am in much pain and will vomit." Peter was surprised and very concerned. He immediately jumped to his feet to help his wife. He comforted his wife and asked for assistance. He showed Helen how much he loved her. Helen began to cry maybe because of the pain or maybe because she realized that her husband indeed loves her and is there for her. His support and reaction to her pain tempered both their hearts.

All was forgotten and forgiven. Love and respect for one another was all that remained. His love for Helen came to the surface as did Helen's love for Peter. They held and hugged each other for the rest of their trip. They were a family once again.

Peter is a spontaneous person in his thoughts and actions. He is easily excited about something and just as easily disappointed. He remembers selectively and selectively forgets. While absent he forgot about his home and thought only of the place he was visiting. As he left the island, he forgot about this place he visited just as readily. As soon as he set foot in his homeland, he remembered all especially his feelings of love for a special angel. She was forgotten for three weeks but now was foremost in his mind.

Dawn finally arrived and Peter was anxious to return to his restaurant. His heart was pounding as he drove and when he opened his car door his legs could barely support his body. He opened the door and entered only to perceive that the interior of his restaurant appeared different as it would to someone that had been away for many years. But truly nothing had changed. It was all as he left it. The walls, the tables were all the same appearing lifeless to him as did his patrons. His employees all ran to his side to greet and welcome him back including the blond haired angel with the blue eyes.

Her eyes dazzled him with their brilliance. His love interest was once again in his view. As she came closer towards him his blood began to boil and illuminated his face. She too reflects the same bright red face. Their trembling lips, warm hands and stimulated body was invisible to others but not to each other. This invisible flame warmed their hearts. The clock told of the passing of each hour and Peter waited impatiently for the end of the work day. For at the end of the day he would be with his love.

It was finally evening as the great force that brings itself up from the depths of the sea to give illumination and warmth to the earth from the sky it must now find its way back to its home for the night so that all can sleep. It is time for all employees to go home and for Peter to accompany his love to her home. Peter is getting ready to leave and Alkmini is patiently waiting for her employer. Three weeks away from him she could not wait to be close to him once again. Her dream of his return is now reality. They are ready to hug each other. Words was not necessary because their souls were one. Peter dropped off his angel and left for his home. Joy on his face. His wife waiting for him and is glad to see his smiling face. She understood the reason behind his happy mood but did not pursue it. She was sure that his love for her had many deep roots. Such a love could not easily be uprooted. His conquests and indulgences here and there have no roots. They might germinate easily but they also wither just as easily for they are not watered by true love.

A month has passed after their return and Helen went into labor. Her mother in law was near her and contacted her husband. He rushed to his wife side and drove her immediately to Astoria Hospital. Soon Peter was given a second gift from his wife, a daughter with her mother's beauty. Peter was thrilled. He stayed the entire night at the hospital by his wife and new daughter's side. He does not wish to leave except when morning came, he realized that he must return to work. He was welcomed back to work with hugs and flowers, especially from his angel, a human flower, that offered him a big and tight hug.

The hug took him to his dreamworld once again. His being filled with love and lust burning through his blood. Evening came and once again he escorted his angel home, holding hands, being close yet never going beyond. Peter kissed her on the cheek and left as always, this time returning to the hospital. It was after midnight when he returned home. He could not sleep thinking of embracing his angel yet thinking of his wife and new daughter. He imagines his angel next to him in bed, embracing her, loving her. It electrifies every part of his body. Divorce comes to the foreground of his mind.

Can he truly walk away from his wife and children? Yet his heart belongs to his angel. Two strong loves, one illicit love and one needed love. What must he do in order to be fair to both women? His choice is a difficult one, but he knows he must make a choice. "Yes, I must decide. I have decided. I will ask Helen for a divorce and marry Alkmini. There is nothing else that will work. I will tell Helen tomorrow about my decision."

Peter is finally able to attain peaceful sleep yet wakes up with a heavy head. He was late. He realized that his wife was not at home but still in the hospital. He quickly dressed and ran to the hospital. His concern and love for her was his focus. He had forgotten about the decision he had made the night before. He forgot what he was planning to tell her. He did not return to work that day but stayed with his wife at the hospital.

Evening came and he was able to return home with his wife and new daughter. The day came and went. The next day he returned to work and as has been his habit now for many months he took his angel to her home. Yet on this evening the warmth he felt next to her was gone. He did not have his usual glow. A tear emerged on the cheek of his beloved as she sensed his coldness. He kissed the girl on that same cheek feeling her tears on his lips. This kiss was not as a lover but as a father kissing his daughter. He opened her car door, and his angel was gone.

The next morning Peter went to work but he did not see his angel there. He was concerned and asked Mr. John if he knew anything about her absence. Mr. John did not know. Peter immediately left for her home. He stood outside afraid to ring the doorbell. He soon left without seeing her. He returned to the store and instructed Mr. John to call her home and find out what had happened. Mr. John followed Peter's instruction and called Alkmini's home. Her mother answered and said her daughter was unwell but would return to work soon.

Time passed but the blonde-haired angel with her blue eyes did not return. Mr. John called her home again as per Peter's request. Her mother told him that her daughter suddenly left to go abroad. An urgent decision for a wonderful opportunity was offered to her. She did not have the time to inform her employers of her decision. The mother apologized for her daughter's actions.

Peter became visibility upset. His eyes began to water for he realized that his dream was now lost forever. He quickly ran to his car and left his restaurant. He drove along the paved pathway in Astoria Park. He parked his car there under the big bridge, sat and cried for a dream lost. Yet he knew it was only a dream and that dreams come and go.

The young employee, whose age difference from her employer's age was almost half, had a deep and well-hidden love for him. She never expressed her feelings to him. He too kept his feelings hidden. His love was always covered by a light veil of affection. But their eyes, like a mirror to their souls, revealed the mutual and silent beating of their hearts. Hearts that dared and could not beat in their two different worlds. Their last meeting took them to a dead end on the wrong road they were traveling on. One heart split from the other and they both left to pursue their separate lives.

Alkmini went away suddenly. She saw the happiness in Peter's face when they met the night before. She knew this joyful face did not shine for her as it did in the past. It shined for another, a normal and stable one was the cause for this new light. It was not from this illicit relationship but from his marriage and home. She did not want to, nor did she try to change it. She simply turned off her own feelings. She allowed herself to remain in the dark, followed by a distant and dim light in the tunnel of a road that would take her to a new dawn. So the young and inexperienced soul left far away and suddenly. She was afraid of destroying her future with an elusive dream.

In England, her mother's brother, her savior, awaited her arrival. He had invited her there several years ago. She remembered him and now wished to follow the path he had promised her. To achieve the courage to follow a new dawn, she went so far as to divide her heart in two. To take one half with her in her new opportunity and leave the other in its place behind. She was hoping that time and distance would extinguish the flame of love in the heart left behind.

As for the employer his love for her did not as easily dissipate. It hurt and the pain was clearly painted on his face. The memory of his angel was alive in his heart and mind and time could not extinguish it. His wife and family would say goodbye to him in the morning and would welcome him home in the evening. He seemed distant and barely spoke. His wife became confused and curious as to the reason for his intense sadness.

She decided to call his trusted friend, Mr. John, for an explanation. He told her everything for he felt she should know. She understood that she was not at fault. It left forever a large thorn in her soul that would ultimately change the dynamics of their family life in a dangerous way. For the time being, Helen was happy that he changed speed down the road he was traveling just in time to avoid the cliff. It would be smooth driving going forward for she knew the personality of her husband and she would work on keeping him on the righteous path of married life.

He is easily distracted but also forgets quickly. She is convinced that he will always return to her. Peter was still inconsolable. His eyes were red and swollen by his many tears. He does not believe that his blonde angel is gone. How could she leave suddenly without seeing him and saying goodbye? Every night he waits at the restaurant until all are gone. He gets his car ready for her to enter. He opens the door of the seat next to him to let his love in so he could accompany her home. He drives to her home, but his love is not next to him. He begins to talk to himself. "Where did she go? When did she open the door and leave? Did she enter her house? I did not see her go in. Is she in there? Yes, she must be there. They told me lies that she is gone. My angel did not leave me. She is still there, inside her house. I know it!! I feel it!!"

Opposite the house of his beloved. The window is closed. Inside is the angel and outside is the lover. He imagines that she can hear him and so he sings with sadness.

> *"Open the window*
> *My blond Vasiliki (a Greek girl who is very loved, very*
> *fun to be around. Everyone thinks she is happy, but she is*
> *hiding her true feelings.)*
> *With your sweet smile*
> *Tell me one goodnight."*

The angel inside with wings on her shoulders opens the window to see her beloved outside. The song is melodic and comforting. She responds.

> *"Do not be angry with me*
> *That I leave for places unknown and faraway*
> *For I will become a bird and I will come*
> *Close to you once again"*

The love that was waiting outside left with some satisfaction. His sorrow was sweetened. She will return to him his blonde angel. He will be patiently waiting.

Every day Peter can be found at the restaurant. His mind is not as focused as before. He is always in a dreamlike state. Nothing no longer excites him. He no longer dedicates all his energy to his work as he did before. Something has changed in his world. The walls inside the restaurant have darken. They have lost their brightness and no longer bring him light. Something is missing and his heart is now heavy. Something has gone from his sight and has ruined his life. At night he cannot sleep for he thinks of his blond angel.

Without her in his life he knows he will no longer appreciate the sunrise and the coming of a new day. All that is left for him is to wait. But what is to come? Can he believe the words the angel sang to him in her song? Can he believe that she will transform into a bird and return to him? He does not know, nor can he hope. Was his angel real or was she just a dream?

His love affair with his employee the beautiful blonde-blue-eyed waitress became a song, and he sent it mentally to his love that went away. She left him alone in the wilderness of fantasy. He sang it over and over again.

> *"So I loved you, like a sweet dream that never ends.*
> *And when I held you tight in my arms,*
> *I saw a new sunrise at dawn.*
> *So I loved you, like a little bird in the snow.*

With my sweet kiss I resurrected you
and I saw the world suddenly grow.
So I loved you, but you betrayed me,
and I continue to live with you,
if it is a dream within dreams a trip to my imagination."

Less than a month later, the employer in love lost his beloved employee. His feelings of love for her, which became a song in his heart and mind, changed. Hate took its place. Why did she leave him? Why did she leave him? He would say over and over again. The bitterness in his soul became another song on his lips:

"There are no angels I must tell you
I thought I had hugged one
What a mistake I made that I would have died for you
Now that it has happened, I know better.

There are no angels. I am no longer fooled
By those blue eyes and blonde hair
Angels always take us to great heights
But we do not have wings to fly."

CHAPTER FOUR: PETER SETTLES INTO FAMILY LIFE

Years passed and the memories faded. Peter forgot about his angel. The misery he felt with loss of his angel had disappeared. The wind picked him up and traveled him forward to a better future. Love, affection, and total involvement in his family is now the norm. Two children in his home that he is responsible for and will care for.

A warm nest prepared for him by his wife with her mastery in home keeping. His passion for the restaurant and business success has diminished. He is no longer attracted to this need for success and his need to be hands on. He passed everything into the hands of his trusted and experienced director, Mr. John. His mother and his wife have become his support and companions at home. To-gether as a family they prepared for the baptism of their daughter.

"Helen, what shall we name our daughter?" "Peter, I have not thought about it yet. We should talk about it." "I would suggest we give her your mother's name. We gave our son, as the eldest child, my father's name. As per tradition, the second child should be named after your family. In particular since it is a girl, your mother's name must apply. Is that not the right thing to do?"

"Peter, right or not, I suggest we make an exception here. I want to give your mother's name to our daughter. Your mother is like my real mother to me. In some ways I am closer to her than my own biological mother. I love her very much and she loves me. I wish to honor her. Our daughter will be baptized with the name Hariklia. It is what I want."

"Well done, you are doing well in making your decisions. Our children will have the names of my father and my mother. No one will be honoring your family but that is because it is how you want it." "I told you at the beginning, whether it is right or appropriate does not matter. There will be an exception here. I want your mother's name because your mother is also my mother." "Okay, as you wish."

In two weeks' time the baptism will take place at the St. Demetrius Greek Orthodox Church in Astoria. A baptism is one of the most important sacraments practiced in the Greek Orthodox Church. The day somebody is baptized into the church is the day that one becomes a Christian, a member of the Church. As in the Catholic faith, baptism is considered the sacrament of initiation. The Godfather plays a lifelong role. The one chosen by the family is Peter's friend, a Greek Orthodox American who is single and is active in his faith.

Choosing a godparent for an infant is something that is taken quite seriously. It is only required that you choose one godparent that is a Greek Orthodox Christian, but you may choose to have two godparents for your child. Selecting a godparent who will be present in your child's life and spiritual upbringing is important to factor in, that is why Peter chose his closest friend whose ethics he knows well. The baptism sacrament has both secular and ceremonial components in the Greek Orthodox faith. The complete immersing of the child might appear strange to the other religious groups even fellow Christians, who made up a part of the attending guests.

Most friends invited were Cypriots and mostly familiar with the traditions. Traditional items that one may choose to include in the ceremony are: Martyrika (a small cross made of ribbon worn by guests, which they can keep as a favor after the event) and Koufeta (candy coated Jordan almonds). Sometimes a special box called a Christening Box is used to fill with the items for the priest to use during the ceremony. These items include: a white bath towel, small white hand towels, a small bar of soap, white candles (two small and one large), olive oil, a set of new white clothing, and a gold cross and chain.

Peter's friend made sure this was done with the recommendations by the priest. These are usually the responsibility of the godparent. One of the traditions that is common to see at a baptism is the Koufeta that is given as a favor to guests after a baptism. Koufeta are candy coated Jordan almonds, often of varying colors, but for the baptism you may choose to go with all white. This is a sweet treat to give your guests as a thank you for witnessing the baptism of your child. You may choose to have the favor bag that the almonds go into personalized.

You can add the date of your child's baptism to the bag along with their name. Peter and Helen chose to offer this to their guests on the tables during the celebration. A Greek baptism ceremony is a special occasion to be celebrated and celebrated it was. This time the party was indeed memorable. Dances and songs of Cyprus, an image of a distant homeland that traveled to the New World.

Peter was melancholy in remembrance of his son's baptism. There were no festivities then. His father's death was fresh, and it was hard to truly celebrate. The only consolation was that his son took on his father's name and was baptized 'Aristides.' Years have passed and the past is indeed the past. Today is here and his happiness must overtake his reflections of events past. Mrs. Hariklia, his mother, happily holds her newly baptized granddaughter, who took her name, in her arms with pride and much affection.

Helen, since their return home, has tried to get Peter to be more involved in family events and routines. Being in church and seeing his Cypriot friends and neighbors once again she was hoping to use it as a foundation to convince her husband to be more active in his faith and this ethnic group. For example, their friends Stauros and Maria. Stauros is a member of the local Association of Cypriots in Astoria. The opportunity now presented itself for her to push her husband to get involved in this association.

"Peter. What do you say? Would you like to get involved in politics, like your friend Stavros?" "What do you mean?" "Yes, to become a member of the Cyprus Association in Astoria." "No. I am not one for such involvements." "But why? You will see that your life will have many other interests. You will make friends. You do not have friends of your own. Apart from Stavros and Maria, who else do we have? You have nobody. Life is not beautiful when you live it in isolation." "Let me be on this issue. We will see if it makes sense for me."

Helen is determined to not give up on this idea. Somehow, someway she will convince her husband to join this group. So she invites neighboring friends to her home. The conversation is about their compatriots, their clubs, their energy in maintaining their culture and faith, their love for their island, Cyprus, and more.

"Stauro, Peter is your friend and we have known each other for many years. We meet many times at events of our compatriots. We always have a good time, but I never thought that neither you nor Peter would be able to be part of the Cyprus Association."

"What do you mean, Helen?" "What I mean is that it would be good if Peter can join your Association simply as an active member." "Absolutely, that would be fantastic. You are so right, Helen. We never thought about doing that."

"Stauro, do not listen to Helen. She does not know what she is saying. The work of the association requires a major commitment of time. Time, I do not have. I work seven days a week and very long days. You are an employee and work only five days a week. You are free on weekends and can focus your time working for the association."

"Stauro, as you can see Peter is looking for excuses. He could if he wanted to he could find the time. One Saturday or one Sunday. The world will not end if he does not go to work. There is someone there that can substitute for him."

"There is no problem. It depends on Peter as to whether or not he wishes to join." "It seems that today you have both chosen to discuss my decision. It is as if you have made a bet that you can get me to be social, which in reality I am not. I know it and I admit it. But you have now convinced me so I will try."

The group was happy to have their friend for the first time in his life join them in the association. The two couples met the following Sunday to swear in Peter as a new active member. Helen was thrilled to get her husband to leave the restaurant, even for a short while. To leave the place that bothers and tortures her. Maybe one day a new waitress will appear, and he will lose his mind once again. She has no clue what takes place behind her back there. Here in the association with all men she has many that will watch, monitor, and report his behavior to her. There will be many witnesses.

Helen's father in Cyprus has been taken to the hospital for a heart issue. He is now in critical condition and his daughter was notified. His concerned daughter decided to be by his side. She left her children with her mother in law and her husband and traveled alone. Luckily, she arrived at his bedside in time to visit with him for within two days he was gone.

Her family missed her, her husband, and their children very much. Her father felt much sadness because his loved ones were so far away. "I am so sad, mama that I have lost my beloved father, but I am blessed that I had the chance to see the happiness in his face when he saw me again. I am convinced that he died happy, and it helps a bit to alleviate the pain."

"My child, your father and I were concerned about your suffering and your agony. You were in our thoughts and prayers every day. How are you now doing? How is living with your husband, now? We discovered your problem when you had visited. We saw your pain, and for us your parents, it was killing us to see our daughter living in such a hell. Has the darkness left your soul finally? We told you then and I am telling you now, Peter is a wonderful man, and he loves you. He will never betray you. Do not risk losing him. Do not destroy such a beautiful family. Do not choose to throw your children into homelessness and poverty. It is a shame and a sin against God to allow such dark thoughts to enter your mind."

"Mama, I hear what you are saying, and I agree. Do not worry. I understand or should I say I know that my husband is wonderful

as you say he is. We get along well together. We have no problems."
"Thank you, my daughter. You have made me happy."

Helen is looking forward to the day when she can return home. In her mind she is constantly thinking about her husband. What can she do now that she is far away? Her mother notices her anxiety but pretends not to understand. Whatever her daughter told her, she was not convinced.

She just does not understand nor believe what her daughter is going through having an infidel for a husband. Instead she believes her daughter is jealous of her husband for no apparent reason. She knows that diseases such as jealousy do not pass easily. They are incurable cancers.

After the forty days of mourning were up Helen immediately boards a plane back to America, to return to her family. Her joy is great as she hugs her children and her husband. She had just about come into her home when she invited her girlfriend to come immediately to the house, just to learn news of her husband's behavior while she was away. And of course if her husband was faithful to the club, its members and most of all to her.

"Helen, from what Stavros tells me, Peter was excited about our compatriots. Almost every night, since you left, he would go with my husband to the club after work to drink coffee and exchange conversations with other friends and acquaintances." "Thank you to God. I was concerned while I was gone, for I left him alone, but thanks to Stavros for accompanying him. Thank you both. You are our really good friends."

Family life for Helen and Peter was finally peaceful and flowed smoothly. Peter devoted his daily hours some to his family, some to his restaurant, and the remainder to the Cypriot Association. Helen was preparing to give birth to their third child. Peter watches over her and helps her in any way she needs. The daily company of their friends provided further stability. Within a few days, Helen was taken to the hospital and delivered a second little girl. Both parents were happy to bring this little girl into their family.

"Now you cannot argue with me. The baby will be christened

Crystal. The name of your mother as per tradition." "Of course I'm not saying anything. I agree and thank you, Peter." Peter, who liked his mother-in-law very much, helped her to come to America for a visit to support her daughter, Helen. So Helen's mother and Peter's mother-in-law are now living with them. She was present at the birth and was also present at the baptism of the granddaughter. There was no doubt that the baby would be christened by their best friends, Maria and Stauros. Maria had asked Helen when she learned of her pregnancy.

Happy is the family as a whole: Father, mother, children and two grandmothers, who were reborn in their purpose in life, rejoice in the names of their two granddaughters. Peter is further vested in the daily workings of the Association and now holds the position of treasurer in the Association. He is more involved in the meetings of the Board of Directors and all of the general meetings, than his friend Stauros. They spend most of the time together. The violent seas are no longer an issue and the family in now in the safety of the port which is quiet and peaceful.

No longer are there clouds in Helen's sky or strong winds in the waters of her bay. Helen is happy. There are signs of recovery from her past that touch her soul. The daily reports of a spying friend are reassuring. But nothing good lasts forever. Her mother now presents a problem. She cannot stay any longer. She has prolonged her visit to America long enough. Helen and her husband have asked her to stay close to them for a while longer, but she cannot do so. She is upset and wants to return to Cyprus as soon as possible. To keep her safe Helen decided to accompany her.

"Peter, my mother wants to leave. She is upset because she feels she must return back to her homeland. I want to accompany her to keep her safe. What do you say?" "What do you mean to accompany her?" "To go with her to Cyprus." "Now? Why don't you wait until the summer for us all to go together?" This proposal from Peter, who imposes himself into the trip, did not ring well with Helen. Her reckless husband should never meet her brother's wife again. She had enough of his infidelity during their last visit.

"Peter. You have your job here and even the association. You must not leave." "But that is why I am telling you to postpone it until the summer. Then it will be easier for me to leave." "No. No. I cannot. My mother cannot bear to stay any longer. Can't you see how stressed she has become?" "Do you want me to talk to her?" "No, there is no need to do so. Please just get us the tickets. We will leave now."

Helen does not like Peter's insistence on going with them. She is afraid of a spark emerging again, of which, as Helen is convinced, did not go out, but instead is buried deep in the ashes of the fire that almost engulfed and would have destroyed her family. "Fine, since you insist on leaving now, I will go tomorrow and pick up the tickets. What will happen with the children? Are you taking them with you?" "No, they will stay with you and your mother. That is what she wants. She does not wish to be separated from them." "Okay, then I will get the tickets."

Tomorrow dawned with an alternate reality. The task of getting the tickets did not happen. The trip was postponed for now. Peter's mother collapsed on the floor that night with a stroke. She was taken to the hospital. Everyone there was upset and waiting for the outcome. Nothing could be done, and Peter's mother was gone. Her death killed her only son who worshiped his mother.

His mother-in-law, who did not leave for her homeland, stayed close to him to comfort him. She was there to remind him that he has another mother who loves him. Mourning is a major burden on any family. Peter, despite everyone's support, is not able to heal. His eyes do not stop his tears. His heart, broken for the loss of his mother, no longer functions properly. Mother and daughter missed the trip for they cannot leave this grief stricken man. The mother-in-law is determined to comfort her son-in-law and heal his wound with the affection of a mother for her child. She has always liked and admired her son in law. He was like a beloved son to her.

There were many times she quarreled with her daughter over her believed unjustified attacks on him. Another month in America for Mrs. Chrisoula would not be a problem. Spring projected onto earth to resurrect the hearts of men. Peter is finally settling and dealing with his loss. The mother-in-law and her daughter decided to travel to Cyprus. They took the children with them to take this burden away from Peter. Peter was left alone. At work and in the Association, he spends the hours of his loneliness. There is no one in his house. His friends welcome him almost every night to their house for dinner.

Helen is in Cyprus. She is sad that she left her husband alone. But she is still anxious that he has moved on from the loss of his mother and will deviate once more. Every now and then she calls her girlfriend to learn the news about her husband. Maria knows her. She knows her jealousy which she sees as an incurable disease. She always reassures her that her husband is behaving himself and is with them every night.

The two friends Peter and Stavros continue their habit of spending every night after work attending the Association. Stauros is a simple member not an officer. Peter as an officer is a member of the board. In the meetings of the board of directors and general meetings, Stavros does not accompany his friend to the club. Since his friend is busy, he does not wish to wait for him to finish. So in these cases he prefers to leave him alone, unaccompanied.

It is the First Sunday after Helen's departure to Cyprus. At the association, the established general assembly is taking place. All members of the board of directors are at the headquarters. Among them is Peter as the treasurer of the club. Down in the hall, people in their chairs are watching and listening to the words and speeches of the leaders of their organization. In the front sits a woman with one leg over the other. The cashier's eye defocused from the numbers and inadvertently focuses on the shapely calves, which provocatively ignited his dormant lust. Lightning in the eyes of Peter.

Thunder in the eyes of the unknown woman. Their fiery eyes met. Stunned Peter left his chair. The assembly is over. People are leaving as the room is now empty. The unknown woman does not leave. She waits indifferently near the door. The unfaithful husband approaches her scared. His cowardice is obvious. This beautiful woman reaches out her hand and invites him outside.

She introduces herself. Her name is Mersini. She is not Greek. She is an American. She once had a relationship with a man from Cyprus and had often visited the club with him. She likes Greeks. It was not difficult for her to confess to Peter and to tell him directly that as soon as she saw him that she fell in love with him.

Peter lost his inhibitions. He did not expect such an aggressive move. He could not resist the temptation and gave readily in. This unknown woman dragged him to her apartment, which was somewhere near the first floor of a large building. There his fantasies and imagination, blinded by the lust that the legs of the unknown aroused in him, made those fantasies become real for the first time. All that Helen feared could happen, indeed did happen.

The unknown woman had learned that the seabass needed to stay in the net. She made sure that they saw each other daily so as to stun the fish so that it cannot see the exit from her nets. The dreamer is in a dilemma. He is forced to be present every night at his friends' house. This was a standing order from his lawful wife with her faithful friend so that she can spy on the movements of the husband that her imagination constantly sees in foreign embraces. This requirement keeps Peter safe from his wife's suspicions.

The couple gives him a very nice alibi, without wanting it and without understanding it. But the days do not only consist of evenings, but also have lunch breaks. The businessman's eye is fixed on the hand of the clock hanging on the wall in front of him. The markers are understood in the number thirteen accompanied by a bell ringing, the sound of which reaches and electrifies another pendulum in the heart of the impatient lover of the day to fly to the nest that traps him. With some excuse to his manager, the employer leaves the store at noon and does not return until the next morning.

All afternoon to eat the forbidden fruit of his new paradise. It did not take many days for the mainland mermaid to fry in her hot frying oil the lucky seabass that she kept in her invincible nets. The unknown woman managed to extract fifteen thousand dollars from the infidel businessman. For twenty-four hours she gave him, in exchange for the gold, her hot embrace. She spread her wings and flew away as soon as she had the money she wanted.

At noon, the next day the impatient lover leaves his job and runs downhill with excitement lingering in his body. He rang the bell of the famous door with his heart beat accompanying the knock. A stranger opens it. The unfaithful husband opened his eyes wide. His gaze is lost on the man's face. The smile extinguished his longing on his lips. The usual vision of lust was not seen at the opening of the door. He did not see his angel wrapped in her provocative attire. He pulled back his body. He looked at the door again. The bell.

Was he wrong? He thought. Isn't this the apartment? Every time he knocked on the door, the mistress opened it, along with the door, and her arms. Why now is there a man? How is this happening? He tried to speak. The words came out confused on his lips. The stranger looked at him with an ironic grin on his face. "Is this the apartment that belongs to Miss Mersini?" "Which Mersini are you asking for, sir? You are wrong. No Mersini lives here."

The door closed behind him. He turned to leave but his eye fell on the wall. There hung a plaque with the names of the tenants. He sees it for the first time. She never told him to ring the doorbell. His mistress told him to knock on the door on the front floor with the number 1A. And he did. On the plaque, however, the apartment with this number was rented to a man. Not a woman. What is going on here? Why did lust and pleasure close his eyes? Where did he go wrong? Why did he not see?

He opened the front door and left. He made sure that he did not make a mistake in the building and in the well-known apartment. He understood that he had been taken advantage of and she played him for a fool. The fairy who he met so suddenly and unexpectedly was not a true fairy. She was deceptive and very cunning. She was the spider that entangled him easily in her web. She was a swindler, with an accomplice, transformed into an angel. She asked him to lend her cash to replenish the amount she lost on a stock endeavor to be returned when her stock went back up. And he believed her so easily, without knowing her, without examining who she was.

He did not even think that the request for cash was suspicious. No, he did not understand. The thunderous love struck him once again. The beauty of the scammer set her trap. She was in front of him like a bee bathed in honey, and he, like a hungry fly, clung to her. The wings of the fly, stuck together, prevent him from flying. The successful businessman, the "loyal" head of the family, left the building. He took to the streets. He does not know where he is going. He is looking to find a strong wall to hit his head.

Helen is still in Cyprus. She is preparing for her return home. The children do not want to leave as yet. They love their grandmother and the friends they made there. Maria in the last telephone conversation with her told her that Peter abruptly lost his temper with her. She continued to explain to Helen about his abrupt change.

Until then he was happy. They had a wonderful time with him every night, but for the past few days he will not talk with them. He has chosen to no longer go to the club. Maria is convinced that Peter is not able to tell his friends the cause of this decision. In the evenings when he goes to their home, he seems very upset and depressed. He refuses to tell them what is wrong when they inquire.

Helen was worried, so she called Peter. The husband justified his grief by alleging that the absence of her and the children was at fault and as such the loneliness he was experiencing. Helen believed her husband, justifying him to her family, and hastened her departure. Her mother could not understand the sudden change she is seeing in her daughter after the last phone call from her friend in America. However, it was not difficult for her to draw a conclusion as to why her daughter was cryptic.

She assumed that "something has happened to her husband again." She is critical and upset about her daughter's psychological condition. Always nervous never at ease, always on edge. She remembers her behavior a few days before when her brother told her that he and his wife wanted to visit them in America. She came up with a thousand excuses and actively tried to prevent them from making this journey.

Her mother knows the cause. Her son has no idea. He does not know about his sister's madness. The mother can no longer stand this situation. Her daughter's misery will quickly lead her to an early grave. She believes that Helen will drive her husband to the same fate. Her heart will no longer endure this misery. She feels this misery deep within her soul. Her daughter needs help but how to help her she does not know. All she does know is that it is all her daughter's fault, all of this, and she cannot any longer support her. This mother certainly cannot understand the pain her daughter is feeling.

The daughter packed her bags as quickly as possible. She took her children in hand. She said goodbye to her mother and brother and left. She arrived on the other side of the world the same day. At the airport, her husband was waiting for them. His face is sad. He could not hide it. The wife fell into his arms, but she noticed that her arrival did not cheer him up. She thought that this separation was responsible for his mood. Now she is close to him again. Where is the return of his joy? Why does his sad face not change?

A new thought now emerges in Helen's mind. Her husband has a problem of his own that is not related to the absence of his family. But what is it? She is determined to find out. As soon as she settled home, she invited her girlfriend over. They spoke, they analyzed the events that mediated over the period of her absence, but they could not find anything that stood out. The girlfriend assured her that almost all the nights she was gone they were with him, except for one night recently. He told them that the meeting at the club lasted very late and so he could not go to their house.

But what is this problem that her husband keeps so close to his chest? How will she know what is bothering him? Is it related to the restaurant? She decided to call Mr. John and see if he knows anything. Well he says he knows nothing. He probably does not want to be involved in her marital issues. She thought of pushing her husband, but how will she get him to tell her. She starts to worry. She is afraid that some new misstep of his will prevent her from every knowing.

"Peter. Will you finally tell me what is wrong with you? What is it that torments you? Nothing has changed in your situation since I came home. It is obvious that you have something that you are not telling me. Will you tell me about your problem?" "What can I tell you? My problem is not about you. It is my problem. I got involved with a scammer and he took my money." "What money?"

"From the restaurant's account. He promised to buy me a building. I gave him the deposit. He took all of it and disappeared." "And what did you do? Did you let him go like that? Didn't you chase him?" "How can I chase him?" "There are courts. To sue him." "How can I sue him? I do not have any proof of our transaction with me." "You do not have it? And how did you give him money without getting a receipt?"

"I trusted him. He wanted cash. As soon as he got the money, he left from the back door. The name he gave me was false. I cannot find him." "Does Mr. John know that?" "He knows I got the money from our accounts. He does not know anything else. I did not talk to him about the rest." "What is the amount?" "Fifteen thousand dollars."

"Well done. Congratulations. What kind of entrepreneur are you? How did you let this happen?" "I do not know. I trusted him." "It doesn't matter. You are neither the first nor the last to be taken advantage of. These things happen when we trust people we do not know. So it happened. Let us forget it." The fairy tale from the husband told to his wife is perfect and believable. He skillfully turned the face of cheating with another woman to that of a man that offered him an unscrupulous deal; a masterful way of handling infidelity that really deserves admiration here.

Unsuspecting and convinced by her husband's words, his wife finally told him to forget about all that had happened. Nevertheless, he did not forget. He continued his depressed mood. The wife's consent to forgive his problem did not change anything. None of her words comforted him. Helen is beginning to realize that something else has happened to her husband beyond theft. Her husband lied to her. The real truth is still hidden. Something new might have invested his brain once again. What to do? She will endure it. As long as it is not a female employee. Let it be something else. She is not concerned. But what if it is what she suspects? Then things will not go well at all.

But what made him leave everything dealing with the club? I wonder if that is where Peter's problem started? How will we know? Stauros did not say anything to her. Is he covering for him? Helen started the secret conversations again with her girlfriend to ask if her husband knew of something that had happened at the club that would upset Peter. Stauros learned from the president and the others that Peter submitted his resignation for professional reasons. That is, he does not have time available to perform his club tasks because of his job. So it seems that no one bothered him at all. If anything everyone there was upset that he left. His compatriots liked him.

"Peter. Please tell me why you left the club. You also had a trusted position there. You liked it. You made many good friends like Stavros. What made you leave it all now? Is there a reason?" "There is no reason other than I am just bored. I told you from the beginning that I am not interested in joining the club. You forced me to join. It was not my choice."

"Yes, but when you were there, you showed me that you liked it. You met a lot of people. Friends who loved you and who you loved. Why don't you like it now?" "You may like your clubs and your compatriots. You were born in the same place as them. I was born here. This is my homeland. I am American, I am not Greek." "Wonderful. Well said. Your parents will be proud of you? You are not Greek. Then what are you? Turkish?" Helen was being sardonic, and her suspicions were now on the rise.

Helen now understood that her husband was not at all well. Something else intervened during the time she left him alone. And that other thing changed him. But what? When and where did this twisted tale begin? How will she be able to find out? Friends do not know anything. She cannot learn anything from them. As time goes on, it occurs to her that the damage was caused by a female person.

The boiling in the blood begins inside her. Her separation brought on by her trip to Cyprus was wrong.

She promised herself that she would not leave him from now on for any reason. Together they will go everywhere. Together so that she can see his eyes where and what they are looking at. To be able to distinguish in his face when he is happy and when he is sad. Peter remains the same in all situations. This adventure cost him a lot. Not so much because he lost money, but because with it he also lost his ability to resist temptation and gained a desire to continue with an extramarital affair.

For the first time he tried a foreign serving, an extramarital sexual relationship. Initially it had a strange taste, different from its usual. Yet with time he liked it. Now he lost her. He must find her or someone else once again. He could not resist looking for this alternative. His wife watched him carefully. She suspected that his anxiety came from such a source. She did not speak to him abruptly. Her behavior showed him much compassion. She wants to keep him in the port that is hers. In the port where his ship is moored and safe. She does not want to let his hands untie their ropes and find themselves unruly in a stormy sea.

A big dance party is being prepared by the compatriots in their Cypriot organization. The two couples that are good friends have decided to attend. Peter is still upset, and he has no appetite for parties. All he wants to do is cry. He does not want to see people. And certainly does not wish to return to the place that gave birth to his tragedy. Helen pushes him to the world that is mixed with two sexes to see his reaction.

She is hoping there will be a representation of the drama behind her husband's depression. She will try to find out the causes of his crime and the crime itself. Friends and their best friends are all at the same table. Music and dancing deafens their ears and strengthen their legs. People are having fun and enjoying their lives. Our temporary life on this earth. "We have a life, and if we do not celebrate it, what will we understand, what will we gain," says the Cypriot song. Maria was taken from her seat by one of the dancers.

She took her husband's hand. Her husband took Peter's hand. Peter took the hand of his wife. They entered the circular dance. They mingled with the others. Known and unknown and soon the dance encompassed all the attendees. A typical Greek circle dance. In particular they danced the Hasapiko. The hasapiko is performed in a line or open circle formation, with each dancer putting their hands on their neighbor's shoulders. So the party continues. The dancers return to their tables. The food and drink continued. Helen is sitting next to her husband. Her eyes are following his eyes, looking for the perpetrator of the murder.

She thinks that the drama that changed the mood of her beloved husband was played out there. But the attempt to get the information failed. This experiment did not succeed. Her plan of mixing her husband with the other sex did not matter. Her husband was indifferent. He is not moved by the attractive figures in front of him. The dance party was over. The two couples returned to their homes. Helen is now sure that the crime did not take place in the place she thought it did. What crime she does not know and is not sure if it is really a crime or the result of a sick imagination. Her disease is incurable as is his.

Her current mental state is unfortunate, for she does not bring peace back to the waves of her sea. Support is needed for both husband and wife. They need to seek treatment. But neither sees their issues. Helen decides she must find a doctor to get her husband out of his depression. She remembered her girlfriend. She went to her house. She wants to share her anguish with her. The pain that kills the life that exists within her.

It is afternoon of the next day and the two friends are sitting in Maria's salon. As they were drinking their coffee Helen started a conversation. "Maria, please help me. I cannot go on anymore. I feel hour after hour I am losing my mind. What is happening to me?" "Helen, you know what is happening to you. You are going down the wrong road. And this road will lead you to a cliff. Stop thinking of your husband as untrustworthy. He is not who you think he is. He loves you and shows you his love often."

"Yes, but now something has changed. He was not as he was when I left. He is different now that I have returned. He told me an interesting story about a theft. But to tell you the truth, I do not believe him." "And why do you not believe him? Do not such thefts take place even today? Why would the man lie to you? We believe him. I am shocked that as you, as his spouse, believes otherwise."

"Maria, you do not know him as I do. Something else is going on. In the beginning I truly did believe him, and I told him to forget about the incident. Yet he is continuing to remain in this state, a state of total hopelessness." "It could be that the man cannot get past this event and blames himself for the loss of so much money. He might need time to forget. Give him the time he needs."

"I said that you do not know him. There is something else going on. Our life together over the many years has never been very communicative but it was fine. But after my return something has changed. He is totally avoiding me and will not speak with me. He does not communicate at all." "Helen this is all in your imagination. It has been created by you. You must trust him, even a little. Peter loves you. I believe that you do not love him. That is why you are torrenting him."

"Maria, you do not know what you are saying. I love him very much, that is why I do not wish to lose him." "I repeat, Peter loves you. It depends on you whether or not you lose him." "I am telling you again. You do not know him. My husband is a hypocrite. He pretends to love me but does not really care for me."

"Helen, forget these annoyances. If you indeed love him and wish to not lose him then stop the craziness. If you continue with this suffocating behavior, he will find comfort in someone else's arms. The man will get tired and leave. You must go with him on a trip together. A couple must trust each other in order to have a good life together. Thank you to God this mutual trust is what Stauros, and I have. You must do the same."

"I do not know. I do not trust men in general and my husband in particular. I do not know, maybe I have become ill. Most likely I have always been ill from birth." "I told you; all will be well. It depends on you. You must try." "I will try, you are right. It depends on me and only me."

The two friends parted. It is now evening, and each are in their homes. Helen is searching her mind for understanding and a solution. Who is indeed at fault? Who poisoned our life together? "It seems to me that everyone is blaming me. Everyone says that I am the one at fault. Everyone, my parents, my friends. Everyone. But why? Why me and not him? They chose to blame me. They do not see what he is doing. Me, without reason, am jealous of my husband? My husband that I love. They say I do not trust him, and I should. They say that I see him as a liar and a cheat. But is he not just that. Why do they not see him as I do? In the end what is the truth? Are they correct, or am I?"

It is not unusual for other women to take sides with the man especially if he is as charismatic as Peter. It is not surprising that other women support the man over the woman herself. More often than not they blame the wife for their husband's roaming eyes. Helen's mother and her best friend Maria should have understood that "men do cheat." Yet they did not support her. Is this attitude inherent in women?

Traditionally women competed for men. Is this why in their eyes men are perfect, rational and the women are considered emotional and hysterical. Helen wonders why she is not believed when indeed she is the one that knows Peter the best. For now she decides to table all her questions and try a suggestion given to her by Maria.

Peter's godparents with their son live in California. They are both doctors and run their own clinic. In the early years when Peter's parents were alive, they had some contact with them, but later for many years this contact was lost. Now, two years later, the contact resumed after the Peter's wish of seeing his beloved godmother again. Helen took the opportunity to follow the advice of her girlfriend: "Take your husband and travel with him, taking him away from this place." So Peter, Helen and their three children traveled to Los Angeles.

The godmother slightly above middle age and her godchild, Peter, slightly below. They found it difficult initially to get to know each other after so many years. Peter was happy once again. The sky appeared to clear for him. It was beautifully blue as the California sky. He laughed often. And with him in this happy mood, Helen found peace again in her troubled soul. They stayed for two weeks. They saw many places.

Helen was enthusiastic about all the sites they visited. Peter was happy. The children are happy. Soon time came and they left California. They returned to their home. Their friends were waiting for them. Peter and Stavros return to their work. Helen and Maria at home visiting with one another. "Helen. How was your trip? I see the change in your face. I believe all went well. Isn't that so?"

"Of course it is. We had a great time. I had met Peter's godmother when I first came to America, and we got married. They are doing well. They also have a very beautiful house and a young son, Leventis. I really liked California. It looks like Cyprus. The sky is clear and blue. The sun is warm and inviting. I wish I lived there. I do suffer from the climate here. Humidity, darkness, and... I am not saying anything else."

"There is not much we can do, Helen. This is where we are and where we live. Good or bad, this is our home We must make the decision to make it work. This place is the least bad for there are places that are worst."

It is December, Christmas Eve, Nick, Helen's brother in Cyprus, wants to visit New York. He has heard how beautiful Christmas is in this big city. He is curious to see a country where his sister has made her home, a country that is fantastic and rich. His mother, who knows his sister's madness, tried her best to prevent this journey. She does not succeed, and the son goes forward with his plan.

The son does not understand why his mother does not wish him to go. His sister did the same when she was on their island and such a conversation took place. The sister does not want her brother to visit her with his wife. Now the sister's brother and the mother's son, in order to avoid discussing it with them, took his wife and got on the plane that takes them to New York, without asking anyone and without getting permission from anyone.

From there a taxi brings them to Astoria. They ring the bell at the door of the house located in Ditmars under the big bridge. They reach the sister's door, with a large plate of surprise to serve. The door opened. At the opening, the sister appears with a black cloud of surprise on her face. The brother hugs her, but the sister collapses on the floor. Her eyes look at the ceiling all night. The visitors were surprised and did not know what to do. They leave their suitcases outside.

The brother picks up the sister and lays her on the couch. She gets up obviously annoyed. The brother does not understand the cause of his sister's fainting. Helen knows and proceeds to try and justify her reaction to him. She hugs them, but her hug is cold. Her lips with difficulty formed her words. "Sorry for what happened. I saw you so suddenly and I lost consciousness. I was not expecting you." "We wanted to surprise you. But I see that it was not right. And we apologize to you." The beautiful wife of the brother answers.

Helen called her husband to come home. She explained to him that they have unexpected guests. Peter quickly finished all he was doing, everything not done was put aside. His priority now was to go home. He took the car and arrived before dark at night. With great joy he embraced both his unexpected guests. A warm welcome to his brother in law and most to his brother in law's wife. Cold welcome from Helen to her brother and his partner.

His heart opened to his guests. Her heart closed to her guests. In the evening all together at the table where Peter made dinner. Helen has a headache and went to lie down. It seems to Helen that her misfortunate fate follows her everywhere and there is no peace. She was happy when she went to see Peter's godparents. Her days in California were always sunny. The cloudy sky had cleared her and remained clear until her return to Astoria. Especially today, black, dark clouds were blown by the wind from a distant island, Cyprus. The dark clouds encompass her soul. What was to be a warm and loving holiday is now a Black Christmas in her heart.

She can no longer stand the madness of her husband. She cannot stand the joy and giddiness that those beautiful black eyes of her brother's wife offers him. Jealousy like a steel rope tightens around her neck and she cannot breathe. She needs to remove herself from this visual that she must endure as Peter's spouse. She seems resolved to experience this torture and not fight for what is hers. He is her husband and must act as her husband. Yet she knows his flaws and feels sorry for him.

But he cheats on her constantly in actions, in words, and in his imagination as well. His thought are always for another woman, not her. He says he loves her but what a perverse type of love is this. Love her but lust after other women, even her brother's wife. She cannot deal with this especially not at Christmas. Her mood will affect not only her holiday but that of her children as well.

Peter is anxious for daybreak to be able to give them a tour of his favorite places. He is not sadden nor concerned about his wife's mood. He does not know how bad it is nor does he care. He does know about her illness, as he calls it, which as time passes becomes more annoying to him. He just ignores her and proceeds with his plans for the day. He proceeds to take his visitors with his car on a tour around Manhattan.

They visit Rockefeller Center and see the enormous real evergreen beautifully decorated with lights. They see all the tall buildings including the Empire State building, buildings that seem to the visitors to reach for the sky. They walked through and had their picnic lunch in Central Park, an oasis in the middle of a bustling city. The city was alive with many people shopping for Christmas. The stores were decorated and animated.

The spirit of the holiday season was alive. Everything excited the visitors. Their last stop was his restaurant, his passion he wished to share with them. He made arrangements for a traditional Greek meal for his guests. They stay in the city until late evening. When they returned home Helen was nowhere to be seen. She did not stay up to welcome back her brother and his wife. She went to bed instead because she became ill the moment she opened her door to her visitors. And now these visitors are in her home.

She is sincerely ill especially since her husband volunteered to be their guide and constant companion throughout their visit. His choice to stay with them throughout their stay has induced a severe headache in Helen. A headache she has never before experienced but now has on a daily basis. Her face shows her pain. Her hatred closes her mouth, and she does not speak. She does not wish to reveal herself and her true feelings. And so she waits although inside she is intensely angry. She awaits for that moment when they will be leaving her home and return to Cyprus.

Peter did not have the opportunity to complete his tour plan for his visitors to take them everywhere and to see everything. A phone call from Cyprus interrupted their visit. The mother of the sister and the brother was taken suddenly to the hospital. The diagnosis was a stroke. Nick and his wife proceeded to the airport, as suddenly as they arrived, to return back to their island. Peter took the final opportunity to take them to the airport and wait with then until they boarded their flight.

Helen has chosen not to want to go with her brother to see her mother. She is convinced that it was her mother's fault that her brother visited her so abruptly without an invitation. She did not stop him. She keeps the anger towards her mother inside her.

The visitors left. For two weeks, she could not breathe. They were finally gone. Her closed lungs opened. Her closed mouth opened. The outburst of rage was forgotten, and the victim was now covered with warmth and smiles patiently hidden for two weeks in the soul of the sick jealous wife.

"You invited them. Who else besides you would do this? Couldn't you live without them? What role do I play here? Am I not here for you? Why didn't you ask me first before inviting them?" "I did not ask you because I did not invite them."

"You must have called and invited them. I saw your excited face and your joy. You did not care about anything or anyone but them. You forgot everything. Your mind focused on them as soon as you saw the black eyes of the woman that enchanted you. Are you not ashamed to flirt with and pursue my brother's wife?"

"Oh! My God! You have become really crazy. Totally crazy. I can no longer bear to live with an insane and unbalanced person that has converted our home into an insane asylum. They need to lock you up there. Eventually you will go to Hell." "You will go to hell, not me. You will be locked up in the insane asylum, not me. You have an addiction to lust and sex, and you cannot control yourself."

The big fight began and even with the doors close the voices were loud enough to disturb the neighbors. The children in the home lost their sleep. Their continuous cries break the hearts of neighbors. The husband is at the door ready to open it in order to leave. The wife does not allow it. She places her body over the door and blocks the exit. She does not let him go. She wants him as her own, her property. She wants him to stay and continue the argument. To be only with her and no one else.

"We cannot live together and apart we cannot live," says a song. Peter turned back and went to their bedroom. He lay down on the bed. His heated brain rested on the pillow. His lips trembled with anger before his sleep set in. His last thoughts were of both of them. "I feel sorry for her, I really feel sorry for her. It is not her fault. It is her illness that is at fault. Maybe I am at fault in that unintentionally my behavior upsets her and aggravates her illness."

Helen lies on the couch wetting the covers with her overnight tears. She did not sleep. She waited for dawn. She got up as if it was just another day. She prepared breakfast for her husband and her children. They all sat at the table. Their eyes met. Wet eyes. Blurred eyes. Dark eyes of insomnia. Their mouths with no speech. They got up from the family table.

A single word left the wife's lips: "Sorry." A word from the husband's mouth: "It does not matter." They parted. The husband opened the door and left. He went to work. The wife was left to continue taking care of the children, and the house, whose walls felt like they were closing in on its occupants.

Helen's brother, Nick together with his beautiful wife, returned to their homeland. The son went straight to the hospital to see his mother. He saw her, but she did not see him. Her eyes were closed, her mouth was silent, her mind was gone. Her heart, ready for the long silent journey, leaves only a few weak beats. The beats lasted for two days. The life clock of the mother has now stopped. The mother died defeated by a hidden sadness she had in her soul for the sick and dangerous situation her daughter lived with which her son did not understand and never learned.

Her daughter, on the other side of the world, mourned the loss of her mother. Her son-in-law, on the other side of the world, was saddened by the loss of his mother-in-law. Sadness and deep sorrow. Two emotions of the soul. They differ in gravity. One lighter, the other heavier.

The years go by. Situations change their positions. The unfortunate wife, who was touched by a severe infliction of the mind, looks like a calm sea. Her mood depends on the air that passes over her. The captain of the ship is trying to save the ship from sinking. But he must know when to open and when to close his sails. If he does not know. If he does not have the experience, then he will lose his boat.

The jealous wife has learned to silently watch the "unfaithful" husband. At their exit from their home. Around people. At celebrations and at parties. Her eyes must now follow his eyes. Where is he looking? What do they see? Where are they focused? To prevent the sinking of her ship, she must have the rudder in her hands.

The "unfaithful" husband feels the rope tighten around his neck. He is choking. He cannot breathe. He wants to open a window and let fresh air into the room to fills his lungs. His wife's illness pushes the air out of him. He spends his daily hours at his restaurant far beyond the stifling walls of his house. As many hours as possible. He returns home slowly, tired, without speaking only ready for sleeping. Assuming he manages to fall asleep.

The sick woman, as time goes on, is not cured. Her passion is strong. Her soul is now empty of any emotion. All around her there is nothing but blackness. Potential threats everywhere. Ready to grab her sustains and her life. She tried to drive them away, but she could not do so. No one near her to help her. She has no parents. She has no friends. With all of them, when she had them, she did not share her problem. She did not admit her pain.

The only girlfriend in her neighborhood, instead of helping her, pushes her further into depression. She believes that Helen is imagining all. She finds it all very tiring and cumbersome. She avoids Helen's company. But the sick woman is looking for the company of her friend, her best friend. She has no one to talk with her. No one to comfort her. No one to understand what she is going through. She is truly alone.

"Maria. Let me talk to you. Let me tell you, my pain." "What can you tell me, Helen that I do not already know? We talk about this over and over again. Your pain is the same. It is nothing new. It is a pain that you have caused yourself." "No. Maria. You are wrong. I do not cause this pain. My husband provoked this pain with his unfaithful behavior."

"Then why do you not leave him? Why do you continue to live with him? Why don't you simply divorce him so you can finally calm down and have some peace." "Because I love him, and I want him to be mine and only mine. But he does not love me in the same way and does not want me to be his. He is not content with just me."

"As far as I know, your husband always loved you and still loves you. You have been driving him away with your madness for many years. He is not leaving on his own accord. If you do not try to find your sanity and see reality as it is, then you will definitely lose him. You will lose him forever. There are many ways a frustrated and desperate person can choose to flee."

"Maria. thank you. Your words have a calming on my soul. Words of a wise person. I will have to admit that I am indeed insane. Only me and no one else. I will continue to struggle to find myself again, to address my mental health issues directly. Please stay close to me. I need your company and advice." "You will have me as a friend but only if and when you find a way to heal yourself. I will wait."

Helen took Maria's words seriously. She understood that her behavior is responsible for driving away her husband. Her husband would never think of leaving if he had a different situation at home. Yet the strong link that binds couples is mutual trust. Only this keeps the balance of love and respect for each other. Without it all is lost. In this relationship this gold chain that binds them no longer exists. She broke it without realizing it through her suspicions and jealousy. He too contributed through his blatant disregard for their marriage vows. Now she is looking for the goldsmith who can repair the weak links, weakened by both of them. Will she find him?

The two neighborhood couples resumed their relationship. They would go everywhere together, even to the club of their compatriots. Helen tried to abide by her agreement to stay calm even during difficult moments, without her usual reaction. She tried to close her eyes not to see where her husband's eyes could be intently looking. She promised her friend and herself. She tried very hard fighting her urges along the way. She grits her teeth to endure and tries not to see the images that others do not see. She wanted to become like them, healthy and not sick. Will she be able to overcome her behaviors of the past? She does not know.

January. New York full of snow and ice. The two friendly families with their children on a cruise ship bound for the Bahamas and the Virgin Islands. Lots of beautiful women amongst the passengers. Peter and Stavros together admire the beautiful ones. Depending on their personal tastes they rank the women as they go by. Helen and Maria are immersed with their children in their own world. The jealous wife cannot stand her husband's behavior. She does not want this anymore, this feeling of inadequacy She promised to her friend and to herself to not feel like this again.

But, without wanting to and without understanding why, she let her eyes follow the eyes of her husband. The same feeling emerged once again, and the anger grew within her like an uncontrollable flame. She tries not to show her girlfriend what is happening to her, but she does not succeed. Her face acts like a mirror clearly showing what is in her heart.

"What has happened to you? You do not seem to be well." "Why do you say that? I am fine. There is nothing that is making me suffer." "Are you sure?" "Yes. I am sure and doing fine." "Fine? So you say. Then why does your face not look like mine? My face shows that I do not care what my husband does or how he behaves towards other women. While your face shows anxiety and turmoil. You must hold on and ignore what you see and what he does. It is the only way to survive."

The dialogue between the two women on the boat, ends with the dismissal of their feelings for the betrayal by their husbands. Helen tries to move on and decided to banish the infection from within her soul. But she cannot. She tries, but she is too weak to restrain herself. No one is there to help her. Her annoyance is not hidden as much as she wants to hide it. In her company of others she shows a false image of herself. An image supposedly harmonious, normal, confidence in living with her loving and devoted partner. She seems to enjoy traveling with him. A trip that resembles a honeymoon for newlyweds. She is restrained. Yet she struggles to calm the stormy sea of her soul. Her illness is not treated with medicine. This incurable disease only leads to madness and certain death.

The journey to the beautiful and sunny islands in the southern hemisphere, the warm part of the earth is over. The passengers depart, and amongst them the two friendly couples, returning back to the north side of the earth. Their environment now turned cloudy and cold. They headed there where their houses are and where their life exists. The jealous spouse opened the door of her house. The walls inside are still holding the contagion of her illness. An illness that does not go away but encompasses the occupants of the family home.

"We had a good time. Isn't that so, my love?" "And of course. We had a good time, my love. But not me, you had a good time with your infidelity, which you cannot seem to control."

"I had a good time with my infidelity, and you had a bad time with your illness, which no matter how much you hid it, everyone saw it and understood it and you cannot seem to let go of it. As you can see, we are a good match. I owe you nothing. You owe nothing to me. Leave me alone already. Do not force me to tell you anything seriously hurtful."

"I have no plans to leave you. I do not care about your insults. I am used to them." "Then what the hell do you want from me?" "To become a human being a good husband. Like most people who respect their families." "Most husbands do respect their wives. There are the few that do not respect them. Then I am amongst the few who do not respect their wives. Can you tell me who you are? Are you one of the least craziest amongst women or are you one of the most craziest who does not respect the peace of their family?"

The life of this unfortunate and diseased couple is still floating on a stormy sea that does not mean to calm down. Even with friends and relatives, a false air tries to stop the waves but with no avail. Between the walls of this house a real and strong wind intensifies the waves dangerously and the boat sinks. The first captain holds the steering wheel, and the compass points the way forward. The second captain is unable to hold the steering wheel and the ship must turn back.

From Astoria to Brooklyn, from Long Island to Staten Island, from New York to New Jersey, from Massachusetts to Connecticut, Greek Cypriots meet on their national holidays, local and national festivals. Parents with their children, grandparents with their families. Greek families who were far from the homeland of their ancestors. All these people open their houses and yards to welcome their compatriots. To speak their language. To sing their songs. To share their lives with each other. Families without problems, are the lucky ones.

Families with problems, are unfortunate. The family of Peter and Helen is unfortunate. The couple cannot breathe together in the same house. The air they breathe is contaminated with the germs of distrust. He wants to escape away, but someone has tied his legs tightly. He cannot run. Someone next to him, who does not want to lose him, keeps him well chained.

The suspicious spouse who promised her friend that she would try to be healed from her suspicions and forget her obsession, did not succeed. She is still unwell, even worse than before. But she hides her obsession from her husband, as much as she can, from her friends and those around her. The infected spouse knows her illness because he reminds her of it daily. In all the little things she does from day to day. Open horizons is where he is focusing his eyes. Fugitive in his own life, this must be his salvation.

"You will lose your husband the way you go. And it can be forever ." Her girlfriend's words echo in her mind. The obsessed woman understood the words and admitted her condition to herself, but she could not be cured. There is no cure for her illness, her lack of trust of him and in all men. It is very advanced at this stage, and she cannot change its eventual progression.

Peter wants to leave, to disappear from this current existence. To become air. To become a cloud and drift away. He cannot stand it any longer. Why such unhappiness in his life? He loves his wife. With love and affection he embraced her with his eyes when first he saw her. Their deep love was mutual for she too had love for him upon first sight. Then why is this union now falling apart more and more each day?

He cannot understand the reason behind all of this. He loves his wife. He feels he behaves properly as her husband, so what is the problem? So he stares or goes after another woman, why is that upsetting her so much? She must understand that he is merely acting like a man. It does not mean he loves her less. In his own way he understands the situation and he knows that it is his own fault.

He justifies her behavior to some degree, and he does not fault her, but he also knows he cannot cure her of her suspicions because he is convinced she does not want to be cured. How can he regain the symbiosis they once had, whose beginning was so wonderful and its continuation now so ugly? "Our fortune and our future remains unknown," say our wise forefathers.

The life of Peter is now so fragmented and uncertain. A sea that changes its wind so much. Peace today. Storm tomorrow. The sea is now his wife. A song on his lips: "You are like a sea, that with your waves you have turned the sea around me dangerous and I am drowning." Peter is frustrated with his life. He is not interested in doing what others do. He is not moved by the joys and happiness of others. His only consolation is his restaurant. He spends most of his day there. He avoids his home as much as he can. There he finds constant judgement. The enemy with the sword in her hand ready for war. A war that can no longer be endured.

Helen spends her days strictly at home. Isolated from friends and relatives. She does not want company. She is hurt by the unexpected encounters of unwanted faces. Everyone who enters her home is a potential threat to her happiness. How can she trust her spouse to behave properly when a woman enters?

How can she have visitors with his addiction? He is addicted to sex, but not with her. She just does not know how to cure him of his affliction. So she has closed off her home and herself to others. Her only partner these days is her girlfriend Maria, who has tried to cure her of her suspicions, but to no avail. They meet almost every day, one at each other's house.

"Helen. As I see it, you are not going to eliminate your madness. Who knows where the madness will take you. I will tell you once again, that with this tactic you will eventually lose your husband. You will make him leave you." "You tell me I will lose him. Are you not saying that I am starting to lose him now? He avoids me. He is not interested in me."

"Well done. You did it. Your man is right, he cannot deal with your whining anymore."

"But what can I do? I do my best for him. I look forward to him crossing the threshold of the house every day. I take care of the children and the house. I am a faithful wife. I do not go out at nights like others. He should be grateful for what I offer him. But his eyes, which are closed to me, are open and engaged for any woman he meets on his way. Tell me, is it my fault that he makes me behave the way I behave?"

"Yes, it is your fault. You and your madness is dangerous. Your mind can not understand how it affects not only you but him as well. You just do not know how to treat your husband. You do not know how to attract him. Every day he sees you with an apron on and one broom in one hand and a sword in the other ready to cut his throat. Change finally! Become more attractive. Men chase a different hem when they are sure and know that their spouse is at home stable and safe. Change, throw away the apron. Dress up to the nines and go out. Show your husband that you do not care where he goes and what he does. Do not create scenes showing jealousy. So you need to shake him up and his interest will start to return to you. Then instead of being jealous of him, he will be jealous of you."

"Yes, what you are saying sounds good, but I am not sure I can do this. It is not me. I am not an actress who can play this role." "Become one." "I just cannot do this." "Then I do not know what to tell you. You are stuck with your fate. I feel sorry for you." Helen's friend Maria was tired of advising her. She understands that her friend is long gone and that one day her way of thinking will lead her to a complete mental breakdown or even madness. Indeed she truly feels sorry for her but cannot help her.

Helen is thinking of a plan. She is thinking of implementing all that her friend advised her to do. Yet she does not have the confidence to believe that she can indeed accomplish her plan. Helen is skeptical but she will try to implement the plan suggested by her friend. She tries, but she does not have confidence in herself. She does not believe she will succeed.

She opened her trunks. Her closets. She chooses dresses. She found something nice that her husband liked during the spring time. Yet they do not fit her because her weight has increased. What a pity! Why does time change the bodies and faces of all humans? What a pity! Why do people grow old and cannot always stay young? The truth is in the image in the mirror. The mirror is never wrong. It shows the real images, after the passing of time. Time which is lost.

Peter came home in the evening. Tired and nontalkative. His wife greeted him at the door with open arms, with a glaze on her voice and on her chest, in a different way from her usual behavior and attire, without the apron, without her negativity, without the sword. Armistice in war. Peace finally as the white cloth was flown. The husband was surprised. He does not remember such a reception happen in the recent years. He raised his eyebrows and he looked directly into the eyes of his wife. The word was formed on his lips:

"What's going on?" "Nothing is happening my love." "Nothing, that is strange." "Why strange, don't you know that I love you. I cannot live without you." "I know that you love me, very much so." "I have been waiting for you so we can go visit Maria and Stavros tonight." "Why tonight? Is there a reason? Possibly a celebration?" "No, just to have a good time. The children are now old enough to take care of themselves and they can stay home alone." "At this late hour. Let us postpone it to tomorrow. I can try to come home earlier." "Okay. I will call and tell them so that they do not expect us to come tonight." Peter cannot understand what brought about his change in his wife. Why this behavior? What is behind this behavior? Why this hasty visit to their friends? What does it have to do with this weird picture?

The next day Peter came home early. His wife welcomed him the same way as the day before. The husband is happy that the war is over. But he cannot explain this situation, this sudden change. Is this the end of a dispute that lasted for so many years? Is it a temporary truce? Is there a trick here that will trap him? He does not know what is happening and so he remains cautious.

In the evening they met at their friends' house. The two men proceed to the living room. The two women remain in the kitchen. "Maria. I started to implement your plan. The negativity and accusations are out. In is sweetness and love. My husband is definitely changing. He sees me again as he had in our previous years. He loves me once again."

"I wish you would stay like this and not start your madness again. I have told you many times, anger, and quarreling, due to jealousy, kills people. It causes divorce in families. I hope, finally, you are focused on keeping the negative thoughts out of your mind." "I will try."

As the evening came to an end their friends and neighbors announced that they intend to leave America in a year and settle permanently in their homeland, Cyprus. Peter and Helen were very upset. They will lose the only friends they have. Their relationship here is a brotherly one that cannot be replaced. They were more than friends; they were a family.

"We decided to leave after many discussions, First of all, the crime in this area is getting worse. There is no safety on the streets and in the neighborhoods. Secondly because it is a good opportunity now that the children are small. If we wait until they grow up, we will go back alone, without them. They will not want to follow us." "You are right. But why? Why leave? Will you have a better time there? No one knows and cannot predict exactly where paradise is located."

Peter and Helen returned to their home very upset. More Helen who likes Maria's advice. She does not want to lose her. Without her who knows if she can keep implementing the plan successfully and where she will end up if she fails. Nevertheless, she is determined to continue with the plan. She visits the shops. She chooses and buys new dresses. She dyes and cuts her hair, uses makeup to look beautiful and young in the eyes of the husband that she loves. The man she does not want to lose.

Peter is now seeing his wife with a different eye. He is amazed and he likes what he sees. The noose that has been around his neck is now very loose. It now longer chokes him. He feels free. Yet what is the reason for this sudden change. He does not know. He cannot find the reason.

The Cypriot Association of Astoria is preparing a dance party. The two girlfriends decide to attend, together with their husbands. Maria was curious to see if the lessons she did teach her girlfriend were still in place. Helen was adorned as never before. Her dress was modern and expensive.

Together the couple and their friends pass the threshold of the open door of the club. The large hall is full of people at their tables. They found their own table and sat in the chairs waiting for them. Music and songs began to be performed by the orchestra. National dances of their homeland began in the middle of the dance floor. The two couples entered the dance. Holding hands with other compatriots, they follow the happy circle.

Peter is hesitant and rigid. He does not know these dances so well. Later the music changed. The beautiful old songs were recalled. A sweet voice from the microphone woke up the lovers. Peter took the hand of his wife and lead her to the dance floor to do the first tango. Stauros did the same with his own wife. The two friendly couples changed partners in the second dance. Stauros danced with Helen, and Peter with Maria. Helen's eyes were fixed on her friend's dance with her husband. The movements of the husband, the tight contact of their bodies and the abrupt turning of her partner's head with his mouth glued to his lady's cheek lit the spark that was temporarily hidden in the ashes of her soul.

"Maria. Peter whispers softly to his friend: I am curious about Helen's sudden change. What happened? Until yesterday she did not want to leave the house. Where does this miracle come from? Do you know?" "No. Peter. It seems strange to me too. We never talked about why she decided to do this now. However, this is pleasant is it not?" (Maria hid from Peter what the two girlfriends agreed on).

The feast is at its height and all the faces are happy. The fun is on the rise. Helen was tired and a headache was the cause. She wants to go home. The others wonder about her sudden illness. But Maria realized that her broken girlfriend could not stand her husband close to a woman, not even a close family friend. They left the club before the festival was over. They arrived at their homes. They said goodbye to each other and closed their doors.

"How is your headache?" "It is still there. It will never pass." "I know. You are sick." "It is you who are sick. And you get sick whenever a woman is near you.." Peter chose not to continue. He went to sleep. Unfortunately, the armistice ended. The war begins again. The clouds darken the sky once again. The blue skies lasted for such a short time.

Helen did not go to bed. She curled up on the couch. The pillows absorbed her tears. This jealousy of hers which does not distinguish between relatives nor friends. This jealousy, which kills her mind and soul she cannot beat. It is invincible. "My jealousy, when I take time to follow it, I find myself going downhill, God himself cannot help or stop me. My jealousy because I love him so very much. My jealousy, with you in my heart is so alive."

The next day Maria called Helen. "Good morning, girlfriend. Did you have a headache?"

"Yes, and of course the same question." "Why? Who else asked you?" "My busy husband." "And where is the wrong? We all know that you suddenly had a headache. The fact is it came on when I was dancing with Peter. Did you see that he bowed his head to tell me quietly so as not to let you listen since you were dancing next to us with my husband?"

She continued. "He wanted to ask me if I knew the reason for your recent change. If I knew anything that I could tell him. That is when your headache suddenly came on. Until then you were having a wonderful time. Only then when your eyes saw the great sin Peter did. Then the blood boiled in your veins and your illness took over your mind. Your sick mind, which will never be cured no matter how many doctors you visit."

"Yes. Let your doctors see me. Like you who I trusted as I would a doctor with the advice you gave me on how to make my husband jealous with my ridiculous makeup and expensive clothes. My husband was not jealous at all, if anything he was glad to have more freedom to go anywhere his insatiable urges takes him."

"What can I tell you? I am sorry for you. Your illness does not distinguish between anyone. Not even your family. I considered you as part of my family. I am sorry for your downward tendency once again. Aren't you ashamed anymore? All I can say is that I am so happy to leave next week and never have to see you again." There was silence on the other end of the line. Helen did not speak. She hung up the phone and the two beloved girlfriends parted their hearts forever.

Peter is saddened by the realization that he would lose his friends. He went to their house the day before they were to leave. He went by himself; his wife chose not to go. He excused his wife's behavior by saying she was ill. Maria tried to comfort him by saying "it is a headache. It will pass." Maria said goodbye to Peter with a sisterly hug and kiss on his cheek.

The next day their two friends Stauros and Maria left. They took their children and returned to their homeland, Cyprus, permanently. In America, Helen is now alone. She has no one, not a single friend, to share her pain with. She does not wish to make new acquaintances. All women are potentially dangerous. She focuses all her attention on her children.

Misery once again emerges from this couple's relationship in the evening. The war continues with no visible end. The children are being raised in a prison like environment with no human contact nor compassion. They are lacking the warm hugs from their parents. They are lacking the love of a happy family. One family that does not mimic other loving families around them. They sit afraid in the corner of their home with the constant anxiety that maybe one day their father will kill their mother or the reverse. Especially during their parents' daily fighting which shows intense hatred of one another.

The parents declared a short lived truce for the sake of their children. They came to realize that these daily battles do not only affect them. They needed as a couple to find a solution. The wife has finally realized that her children are suffering and cannot deal with these daily battles. She decided that she must end the war which truthfully did not start totally on her own, for her children. In such a home there are no victors, no one is victorious, there are only traumatized souls.

The husband over the past few years has chosen to spend more time with his family. In the evening he takes his children to Astoria Park. On weekends they take a car ride out to Long Island. The eldest, Aristides, is now close to ten years old. The mother is focused on him. She needs to help him. She is trying to heal his battle wounds which she and her husband inflicted on this child over his ten years.

Yet the time with his family is shifting to his old focus, his business. He is giving his business the same personal involvement and enthusiasm as in the past. One of his two waitresses gave her resignation for personal family reasons. He chose to do the hire and found a younger and more beautiful woman to replace her. His heart began to beat faster once again when he laid eyes on her. His heart was awaken from its slumber. His reaction to his new waitress was immediately understood by his wife. Many years of practice. The firing of the guns commenced, and the war began once again.

"What is wrong with you? Can't you live without being surrounded by women? Are there no men for these positions? The vacancy could have been filled by a man. Your father hired men. What is the difference? Is it not best for you to do the same?" "I am not involved with the hiring of staff. Mr. John is responsible."

"Mr. John was the manager under your father and did what your father ordered him to do. Do not tell me that now he makes his own decisions. Do not try to hide behind Mr. John. I know you all too well. It is in your blood, and you will never change." "Once again you are starting with the same suspicions. When will you get the help, you need?"

"It might be best at this time not to engage me further. This way we will have peace from one crazy and ridiculous woman." "Then you should go and live with the crazy street people that I would suspect are more mentally stable than you." The husband chose not to continue so he slammed the door and left. The children could be seem back in their corner afraid and crying over their parents' dramatics. The mother forgot about protecting them. Before their wounds healed from the last battle, new wounds were inflicted. The same battles carry on and will never end.

Helen made a decision. She just cannot live this life any longer. She wants her freedom. She wants to leave so desperately. Inside her is a force that is preventing her from doing so. It will not let her be. She does not know what to do. She has doubts and cannot make a rational decision. She is living in the same prison as her mate. They are toxic for each other. Yet she cannot leave him. She cannot live alone. She needs him. She knows that she loves and hates him simultaneously.

What can she do? She no longer has friends near her that can advise her. No one wishes to be her friend and in turn there is no one she chooses to be her friend. But why? What is the reason? Maybe she is indeed crazy? Maybe her husband is correct?

Her head is dizzy, and her nerves are shaking her body and mind. She throws water on her face to recover. She remembers her children. She takes them into her arms. Together they arrive at the nearby park. The children play on the grass, how easily they forget. She is sitting on the bench thinking. There is no solution to her problem. She admits her illness to herself. Jealousy in her soul became her passion. Passion so strong and incurable that it is destroying her life. Passion that finally only leads to madness and suicide. Which of the two will she be able to choose?

She decided to take a trip to her homeland. She left the children and her husband behind. She left alone. She closed her eyes and ears to all and chose not to see. She does not wish to listen nor imagine. Maybe far away she can be healed.

She arrived at her destination. Her parents' house was deserted. Nobody lives there anymore not since the death of her parents. Her brother and his wife live nearby. She went there to be with them. The brother was ecstatic to see her, and his tears warmed her cheeks. The brother does not know and will never know about his sister's illness. The bride does not know and never will learn that there was once a smidgen of scandal from her "unfaithful" husband, who "fell in love" with the bride.

The first warm days of her visit are over, and the sun again is gone, and clouds darken her sky. Her imagination paints images of times that clearly show her husband in the arms of the angels of love. He is with young women once again. She wants to get out of there again. To turn back. She cannot stand away from him. She wants to be near him so as to see where his eyes are looking. The beauty of the angels he admires. Her husband had no objection when she announced her decision to travel alone. He did not stop her. He thought that it would be good for her to be away from home and family. He would take care of the children both at school and at home. But she misunderstood the consent of her husband.

Why didn't he stop her? Why did he want to be alone? So what was his reasons? The sick woman's imagination paints images in her passionate mind that kill her tired soul. Get out as fast as you can, she thought. To prevent evil. So to the airport she ran. Before she realized it she was found on the plane. And that brought her back to the place of her martyrdom. Where her life continues with ups and downs on the raging waves of the sea.

The mother hugged her children again, but the children were hesitant, because for the time she was away, those children lived a life without storms. The wife found the husband again, who welcomed her happily because he missed the war he was so used to. The children are afraid of their mother's return because of the potential of a new collision of the two opposite poles and the fire that will burn their small and innocent souls once again.

The husband, tired of captivity, seeks his peace and freedom. The husband laid down his arms and attempted to capitulate to the enemy camp. Will the negotiations bring results? Or will they fail? Will the war end? Or will it continue until the final annihilation of all wars? It depends on the secret plans of both sides.

One day Helen picked up her children and traveled with them to arrive at the restaurant by train. She wishes to see with her own eyes the eyes of her husband and upon who he was staring at. All were surprised when they saw her and the children. She was afraid of repeating the story of the previous young waitress with the new young waitress whose imagination easily shifts her into the arms of her thirsty employer.

Peter understood his wife's intention for the sudden visit. He tried and succeeded in showing to his suspicious wife his alleged indifference to the female waitress that was near him. In the evening they all went home together. At night, as if they were alone, with the children lying down and sleeping, the implications of the incurable jealous partner began: "I see your new employee is very beautiful."

"Why does that matter? Is she the only one who is beautiful? They are all beautiful there, both women and men. And none more beautiful than you." "No, you can't compare me to her. She is beautiful and she is young. I cannot believe you do not like and most likely enjoy seeing her every day? Besides, you always have a preference for beautiful and young women. You have proved it to me over and over again."

"Must we do the same again. You are giving me a headache. Please stop your complaining. We can discuss all further when the dawn breaks, not now. Turn off the lights so we can sleep."

The next day dawned, but the couple did not choose to discuss the topic further. The man opened the door and left. The woman accompanied him to the door with the prompting to hurry up and go. And the man left for his restaurant thinking not only of his own weakness, but also of the headache that would not leave his head caused by his beloved wife the evening before. One day it would be light, without the loud complaining. One day it would turn to dark with the complaining in the background.

The hours and the days pass. The couple lives their life on a sea, which changes its waves depending on the air that passes over it. Sometimes the waves were calm and sometimes there were storms. Their ship would sink to the bottom, and then it would rise with the foam. It is difficult for them to be ruled by divergent actions. They would constantly miss the shore because they could not the steer the wheel. One of them does not trust the other. One spreads the sails of the ship. The other closes them. And the ship comes and goes. Their ship stays in the same position never sailing to the open sea, nor does it reach the port that will protect it from winds and waves.

The employer of the restaurant had to learn this lesson because he dared to link himself with his employee sometime in the past. Today another employee, similar to the previous one, attracts the boss once again. But he wants to stay away. To keep the distance, despite all his inward desire to zero in and capture this bliss and ultimately repeat his previous behaviors. In the past, the husband was guilty. In this second case it is not as clear. What her eyes saw is hard to explain. What they did not see and do not see in the end does not matter. All he wants now is that they remain just the suspicions of a jealous wife who creates beautiful images in her sick mind.

In the evening Peter returned to the house. His wife, remorseful for what she had told him the day before, welcomed him warmly. The wind changed direction. The serene sea caresses its shore. At night, the husband, soaked by the waves, dries his clothes in her warm embrace. The warmth of the embrace warms the soul of both husband and wife. And the soul sings the love of the wife to the husband:

> *Come sweetly and kiss me*
> *Turn off the light and hug me*
> *We will not find any edge*
> *Turn off the light to sleep*
> *When dawn comes, we will say it again...*

Life for the tormented couple continues peacefully from nowhere. How long peace will last depends on many things. Peter tried to hide his feelings when he met females on his way. He was tired of the war at home, so he chose to behave. He wants to avoid the cause. Helen, reassured by her husband's indifference towards other woman rests on her laurels. She now lives in an ordinary family. She hugs children once frightened by previous wars.

The wife now takes on more work. She takes care of the family budget. The wife is at home. She takes care of their children, particularly their education. They are together as a family in the husband's free time. On weekends they attend church as a family and spend time together in the neighboring park. The woman's illness has disappeared. The infection, she had now found its antibiotic. Is there a fear of such an infection recurring?

It depends on the germs that the wind will carry, and time will only tell. From the translator: From a movie called Star Trek Generations - my favorite definition of time spoken by Patrick Stewart as Captain Picard. "Time is a companion that goes with us on the journey and reminds us to cherish every moment because that moment never comes again. What we leave behind is not as important as how we lived." Let us hope that Helen and Peter have understood this importance.

CHAPTER FIVE: THE RETURN OF TEMPTATION

The blonde angel with the blue eyes admired by Peter was now living in England. Suddenly the elusive dream left, which did not realize that her employer was as much in love with her as she was with him. The beautiful daughter went to live with her aunt and uncle. There, in this distant land, she buried her dreams.

New world. New people. Different life. She took on all new experiences and was willing to spread the veil of forgetfulness in order to move on. And he too had forgotten his angel as time passed. Yet he did not forget her in his heart, where time cannot dwell.

Alkmini went to her relatives, far away from this potentially dangerous experience, to extinguish the dream before it became her reality and would lead ultimately to a catastrophic future for her and for Peter. A new life, full of love and affection, welcomed her. Her aunt and uncle had no children. The niece filled their hearts and their arms. They considered her their own child. They send her to school to continue her education which she interrupted when she left Peter.

This is where her fate changed. She met a middle aged teacher at the High School. More than the someone else she had buried in her memory and more so, this man is alive and here. The image of a forgotten dream on the teacher's face illuminates a new dawn. The professor of Greek literature, although he is approaching his middle age, did not have time to build his own family. He saw a light in the young girl's eyes.

A star that showed him the way he had not encountered until then. The young lady with her blond hair and blue eyes found the dream she lost once again. A dream that now may not be a dream. In the free embrace of the teacher she will feel an embrace that she could not rejoice because he was not free. The middle-aged teacher felt a strange agitation in his soul, facing a new student in front of him. Her eyes, like wide seas, traveled him to unknown, dreamy worlds. He noticed her. He forgot her. He approached her. The girl accepted the attraction she felt. An attraction similar to another that was lost. They spoke. They walked together. They agreed on a future relationship.

Alkmini spoke to her aunt and uncle about her teacher. She did not reveal her feelings for him. She asked them for permission to receive him at their home to meet him. And one day the middle-aged teacher with the gray temples passed the door of the house that hosted his chosen student. The aunt and uncle met their niece's teacher. Their impressions are good and accepting of a highly educated man. The teacher also left happy for his student's family liked him. In the evening of the same day, the niece spoke to her aunt and uncle about her feelings:

"Aunt. What do you think of my teacher?" "Why, my child? Why do you ask? Your teacher is a very good and decent gentleman." "Aunt. I want to confess something to you. It may seem strange to you, but I have to talk to you." "What? Alkmini, what do you want to tell me?" "I love this man and I want to marry him." The aunt was holding the edge of the table, ready to be knocked to the floor by a strong blow to the brain. The niece helped her sit back in the seat. She recovered.

"What did you say, Alkmini? Something you said. I think I heard you correctly.. Do you want to marry your father? Because this man is the same age as your father. Is what you say true?" "Yes. aunt. It is true. I want to marry him." "Are you crazy, my child? You are a young and beautiful girl. So many young people would like to meet you and with time marry you. Why are you in a hurry? This man carries double your age on his shoulders."

"I want him, aunt. I am not moved by young men I meet. Young men do not know how to love, not as well as those who are not young. I want romance not just a physical relationship." The aunt talked to the uncle. She notified her husband's sister who is also the mother of their niece. And the mother got on the plane and arrived in London. As soon as she arrived at her brother's house there was a family council. The mother announced that her daughter must be crazy. The same issue emerged when she was in America.

Her daughter chases older men, loves only old men. Isn't she crazy? she thought. She escaped from one relationship only to fall into another. Despite all this, the mother chose to meet her future groom, who also seemed to be her peer. She realized that her daughter had a deep problem. This action is a reaction of her heart to the previous desire that was left unfulfilled and that the same heart revives that forgotten desire in the face of another man, similar to the previous one. The daughter is adamant. She will not change her mind. The mother and the others retreat. The wedding took place. The crowns exchanged between the blond and gray heads. And the bride settled into her husband's home, an image of her father.

The years passed. The daughter with blonde hair and blue eyes took her husband and they arrived in America. In her place. There is still the dream that is alive in a secluded corner of her heart. She knows where to find him. At a restaurant in the Bronx, her former employer. The door opens and through the threshold passes an odd couple hand in hand. At first glance they look like a father and daughter. Peter, the restaurant owner is still there.

Time did not change him much. He opened his eyes only to close them quickly. A bright light hurt them. He opened his eyes again. Clearly in front of him a dead dream came to life. In this middle-aged man with his angel he sees himself. Yet it is not him. Sadness and joy. Joy and sorrow are his feelings. The same feelings of the angel who flew near him once again. Her joy is clear for she wished to see him. Sadness also appeared on her face for she did not have him. The young woman falls into the arms of her first middle-aged love. The passion is obvious and fiery.

She lit the first spark in the soul of the second middle-aged man and husband. Flame and fire unprecedented for the former bachelor. The husband does not know what it is that suddenly shook his heart and struck him. What to do? Is he in love with someone he has secured? Yet is he afraid of losing her? In front of him there is a thief trying to steal his treasure. He resists the desire to attack this thief. He struggles to chase the thief away.

Instead he spreads his wings and covers his treasure. He does not allow anyone to take her from him. His treasure is his. Only his. He acquired her legally with a priest and a best man. He had the right to fight this thief and protect his marriage and home.

Peter invites his visitors to his house. His wife recognizes her former rival. A sharp pain in her heart stimulates her mind. The sleeping germ wakes up in Helen's mind. Looking for entry into her bloodstream. Infection is approaching. Jealousy is reemerging. Next to the young lady a middle-aged man. Could it be her father? Why did they come here? What do they want? Helen is beginning to get upset.

The introductions proved that instead of being her father this man was her husband. The former young rival married someone who matched in age to someone she once met. Helen's husband, which Helen knew, was Alkmini's first and only love. Yet Helen was happy with the situation. She learned that this woman is married. Thus the threatened danger no longer could exist.

Later, a thought came to her mind: Many times young women marry older men in order to inherit their fortune, in exchange for love. In this case, the young woman's husband is not rich. He is a simple teacher. Payroll limited employee. Why did she marry him? Who did she wish to replace? When she is in the arms of this older man, does she not wish to feel the embrace of another older man she loves? And is this other one, the one who she cannot forget, the one she came to see once again, holding the hand of someone else, to show him how she holds his own hand? The passion of the former employer and the former worker find each other. Their faces are a mirror of their souls. The jealous spouse felt the passive germ come to life again. Infection in her blood impedes its normal circulation. The spouse and her husband violated the armistice. The war of this couple reemerges.

She would not allow the boiling of her soul to come to light and be seen by him. She retreated and delayed the restart of the war. Her hope is that the enemy will retreat on her own without the need for artillery shelling and bombing. She is waiting patiently on the embankment.

Visitors from England show no signs of leaving the place they visited quickly. One of them has a permanent residence in this place. She was born there. His parents are here too. The parents and their daughter hosted their new son-in-law in their house. The daughter is visibly happy. Happy that she returned home and that her secret and eternal love, which she did not forget, lived in the midst of it. The mother understands the joy of the daughter. She is afraid of seeing the black tail of the cloud that hides an upcoming tornado.

In the Bronx, the newly wedded couple go every day for a meal. It fills her stomach with food and contents her eyes with love. The foreign spouse reluctantly accompanies his spouse. He is not in the mood to be there every day. He does not like the food, nor the cook who cooks it. He wants to change places, find a new place to eat his meals. He wants to leave. The annoying joy of his young partner when they approach the restaurant frustrates him.

The passive germs in his blood come to life. The wind carried them from somewhere nearby. Someone else infected transmitted the disease to him. The wife of the happy and cheerful owner of the kitchen has those germs. The English infected spouse and the Greek infected spouse are now allies in this war. They both decide to declare their feelings to their spouses.

The English gentlemen, Mr. John, approaches his wife first. "My love. I am tired of this place every day. I want to get out of here and visit somewhere else. We have stayed here long enough. You told me that our visit would be for a very short time. But I see that you do not want us to leave. Why?" "I do not understand. Don't you like it here? You have not seen anything yet. This country has much beauty. We will go everywhere soon."

"Shall we go everywhere? Where is everywhere? We only go to a restaurant every day. Is this the everywhere you are talking about?" Soon Helen approaches her husband: "But your guests have not left yet? Did the temptress who drove you crazy in the past decide not to leave you? Does your madness give her some hope and allow her to dream of a life with you? Is that why she does not wish to leave from here?"

"What happened to you again? What are you afraid of? The woman is married. She is not doing anything." "And you are married. But you do a lot. Marriage is not a shield for the insane."

"Oh, just go to hell. I cannot stand being around you anymore." "I would suggest that you go to hell. That is your future place of eternal residency."

Several days have passed. The guests decided to finally leave. The two allies disbanded their alliance. Everyone in their appropriate place. Temporary truce for both couples. Although a truce, the generals do not lay down their arms. Reclassification and a temporary truce is part of their military strategy. They are always ready to face new dangers.

The middle-aged man from abroad is also infected. He inherited the infection from the place he visited. There is no antibiotic for him now. His illness is for life. It hurts him continuously. Mr. John is jealous of his wife. He never leaves her alone any longer. He accompanies her on her outings and watches her every movement. The young wife is indignant. She cannot stand the tightness she feels in her neck. Like a noose tightly on. She is choking. She wants to leave, to break her bonds with someone who suddenly became her tyrant and terrorizes her. She is thinking of leaving. But where to go? To the man she loves and never forgot? He is not available. He has a family. He has children. The same reason that made her to leave and emigrate in the past is still relevant. No, she will stay where she chose to live. She will simply try to see the face of her lover in the face of another in the framed portrait of the wall opposite her.

The middle-aged husband of the restaurant cannot stand the infection of his wife, who has been infected for years. He too is choking. He cannot breathe when the air is full of germs. It takes his breath away. But it is a chronic disease. And its presence is familiar. It changes direction many times. The germs come and go with the environment. The sad truth is that Peter has become accustomed to his wife's changing moods.

Her jealousy has no end, but it has times when it solves itself. For now everything is quiet again. The threatened danger has passed. The unwanted couple is gone. The sky is clear, as long as the wind does not change, and a black cloud of lightning and thunder appears. At work the husband is content. At home, the wife is content. The distance is large between them. The simple eye does not see the truth in this image.

One would need strong eyes. But even these do not help inside this strange relationship. So Helen continues on her quest to spy on her husband. The jealous wife calls the store every now and then to find out where her husband is. She does not trust him. Various strange and suspicious visits is her answer to her distrust of him. The sinful and guilty spouse is getting tired. He cannot stand her constant monitoring. His problem remains. It does not change. His partner simply does not believe nor trust him.

"I do not believe that your temptress has left. She came here to show us that she is married so I would feel secure that she is now safe. You are lying, you always lie to me."

"What is happening to you once again? I am telling you the truth. They have left and are no longer here. I swear to you. I am not interested in her. Only you do I love. How many times must I tell you?"

"I do not believe you and do not swear to something that is not true. Do not try to hide through your empty words. I do not want you to tell me anything more. Say those empty words to someone else." "Why do you not believe me? I am telling you the truth, but you are too jealous to see it. You see everything suspiciously and you have made life a constant suffering for me." "Whatever you tell me I do not believe. Say your words to someone else and do attempt to convince me." The life of these companions who once decided to live together through love is a tumultuous sea. One minute the waves are ferocious and the next they are calm. The wind that passes over the sea changes the height of those waves from a simple ripple to one that can only lead to death. The life of this unfortunate couple drifts from hell to paradise and back again. A sunny day followed by a dark and cloudy one. No stability nor predictability.

Peter met Helen on a beautiful island. Twenty-year-old children that fell in love and got married. Their love had deep roots and still does. Nothing has uprooted it. However, the soil that covers the roots is severely contaminated. Germs are the cause. Medicine needs to get into the soil to kill the germs so that the roots of love do not dry out.

Is there a drug? If there is, is it enough? Yes. There is medicine and it is enough. It depends on the individual who will use it to be successful. Germs that is jealousy. Medication that is trust. Trust kills jealousy and brings the infected couple back to the paradise they had once thought they had lost.

Helen was silent. She must stop her suspicious nature and her espionage. It does not lead to another good nor does it go anywhere. She admitted that all evil is created by the disease of her soul, jealousy. A disease that cannot be cured and cannot be removed. Love and jealousy are sisters. Inseparable sisters. They go everywhere together. The greater the love, the greater the jealousy. The jealous individual loves a lot. Helen is one such individual. She is very jealous. These two strong senses shake her soul. They curse her heart. Less love. Less jealousy. Maybe the injuries would be less for both her and Peter.

Helen remembered the words of her girlfriend while they were neighbors "To show her husband that she does not care what he does in his private life. That is, she does not feel jealousy. She does not envy him." So she decided to make a change in how she handles her feelings. "No, I must try this time. To love less, so that it can hurt less." She will try, even though it is difficult for her and maybe even impossible. Such a thing is not governed by logic.

It is controlled by her soul, by emotions. And the soul is independent. She must take the opportunity to limit the wind of hate and disappointment. She will no longer carry those clouds with her for the hours she spends with Peter. She will warmly welcome her husband in the evenings. She will part with her partner in the morning with a smile. Words spoken count. Calm and pleasing phrases only. Smile constantly on her lips. Happiness in the heart and in her motions. Sweetness in her eyes. That will win him back. She is sure.

Peter was surprised. The behavior of his wife took him back to a beautiful island bathed in the clear blue waters of a warm sea. Where he found love. There they were both alive. Dead now. But life tried to overcome death. Dead love is finally revived. The binds that held him have been untied from his hands. He can freely hold the oars of his boat that brings him back to his secluded port, without the strong winds that he could not fight.

The changing behavior of his wife was a welcome. Where did her tedious and destructive jealousy go? Did it truly leave? Will it come again? Did her illness get better? Is what he sees a miracle? But are the miracles happening today seem odd? He does not know. The fire has been extinguished. The spark remains. Under the dust there is always a spark. He is afraid of this spark. If it is not dead, it easily can become a flame which can turn into a full blown fire that burns and destroys all around him. He is afraid to do anything that can stir the ashes to reignite the flame. If you stir it enough it comes to life.

The shuffling was caused by a hand. And his hand is the only hand that can reignite that flame. Every war that becomes a truce starts again for some reason. The cause here is his behavior and the reaction by his wife. He was tired of the war. He cannot stand it. He wants it to end, and she wants it to end too. He decided. From now on he will avoid the cause. This way the war will end.

Helen wanted to visit her place of birth. It was just about her place, not about visiting her relatives. Her island is beautiful with the blue sea and the dreamy beaches which she longs to see again. She wants to travel back to her homeland once again, but this time she does not want to be alone. She wants the whole family to accompany her. The problem is her brother and his young and beautiful bride. She remembers and is afraid of the lust in her husband's eyes when he sees her. She will risk it. After all, it is her decision, and she made the decision to go. Now she does not love him that much. Love him less. That is something she could do.

Summer has arrived. The whole family is on the plane. The couple with their three children travel to Cyprus with much peace. The children are finally happy to see their beloved parents getting along. They have chosen to drive their fears of the past away. The children were excited to be in a different place than the one they know.

The family ended up in a hotel in the island's capital. Helen now faces a dilemma: Should she meet with her brother? Will the encounter help her or make her sick? She promised herself that she would love less. Maybe this is a medicine that will give the strength to get through, even for a while. She does not know what her partner's eyes will do. Will the flames of lust be ignited, or will they remain as extinguished coals? She does not want to know. She will not oppose them if they do. She will try to tame her feelings. Her jealousy.

She decided to call her brother. The brother came to the hotel and took them to his house. The young bride welcomed them with open arms and sincere brotherly love. The guests are timid and very cautious. Peter keeps his personal promise: "Never again will I be the cause of war." Helen her own personal promise: "To love less."

Two personal promises that neither one knows the other had made to preserve the relationship of the spouses of this troubled family. The husband hugged his brother-in-law. She hugged the bride. The two camps facing each other. The eyes of the husband did not catch on fire. The cannons of the wife did not fire. The capitulation succeeded. The war was forgotten.

Visitors from America stayed on the beautiful and warm island for about a month. They went everywhere, visited many beautiful sights. They enjoyed sunrises, sunsets, and the rising of the moon. They had dived into the clear waters of the Mediterranean. They filled their lungs with the fresh air from this blue homeland and returned to their home in America re-baptized in the pool of peace and tranquility. The medicines helped. The disease has disappeared. Life has changed for this family. The whole world was beautiful once again.

Two months passed after their return from the trip, Helen became very ill. Severe abdominal pain forced her to be hospitalized. Anxious and very concerned, Peter was with her at the hospital. Next to her in her room. Both day and night. His new re- baptized soul in love, shows him the way. Helen received his message. She is sure that her life partner loves her. Love. True love is hidden in actions. And only in the actions, not words. Peter stays there holding her hand, comforting her. Love adorned with roses and words of romance, is wispily floating in the air. The air takes it, and it gets lost.

Helen has been in the hospital for a week. Her spleen was removed. The pains were soon gone, and she returned to her home in the arms of her husband, who truly loves her. Her life found its way back to a better time. A clean road ahead without any obstacles. The quarrels are over. The jealousies are gone. The children are smiling once again. The family rolls peaceably on the solid rails of love.

Peter has returned to his restaurant and is there every day. He takes care of everything. He controls everything. He is a serious employer in his relationships with his staff. Restrict and imprison his wandering and disobedient heart. He allowed his logic free and to guide his actions. At last life is good. His wife seems to have been cured of her illness both body and mind. He does not want to see her sick again. It is too dangerous for his family. Yet his new young waitress raises his blood lust once again. His pulse is running non-stop.

He must control his urges, so he presses the brakes of the heart hard. He does not let her tempt him. He promised himself to avoid the cause. The one that brings wars to his household. He does not want war anymore. He is tired and loves the peace he currently has. He wants that daily peace and love. And for the time being he has it. He pays attention to his lustful and wandering eyes. Remove from them the glow of desire, so that the eyes of his partner does not notice them when she visits him and finds him surrounded by the woman of his restaurant by choice.

Meanwhile Alkmini in England can no longer suffer the jealousy of her husband. She is choking in the noose that he has tied around her neck. She has decided to seek a divorce from her middle- aged husband. He told her he does not want to come back to America. She loves her former employer very much, yet she does not wish to ruin his family. She knows that if she meets him again, and is indeed free, he will sacrifice his wife and children just to be with her.

She saw when she visited him his ebullience the moment he saw her, and his longing to be in the place of her husband, the teacher. She does not want to meet him again. She does not trust herself for she knows she will indeed bend to the weight of love and desire. She left the marital home. She did not accept the apologies and pleas of her husband with the gray temples. She knew him by now.

The scenes are the same, despite the apologies and promises. Jealousy is a disease and cannot be cured. She could not stand it any longer and so she left. She finalized her divorce. She found a job and stayed in this country. Away from everyone. Away from middle-aged dictators of love. Love must be freedom not imprisonment. She does not want to be enslaved. To be sold in slave markets. She loves, and will always love, the man she once met in a corner of the big city of the world.

The man who spoke to her soul and woke up for the first time the strings of her heart. The man who united two feelings in one set: The love and affection of the father for his daughter and the love and lust of the man for a woman.

To this man. In her first love, she will remain faithful and wait......

The more it unites us, the more it divides us.
And I do not know anymore what to say.
The more you win, the more you scare me.
I have forgotten how to love.

And it is a pity that you are not
in my life now.
And it is a pity I do not have
your warm hug.

And I do not want to leave you
nor to turn back.
I know nothing is as
it was once.

So many questions,
without answers.
And I do not know anymore
what to think.

You have left behind
so many memories.
Tell me first
what to remember.

CHAPTER SIX: FIRST LOVE REIGNITED

Many years have passed. Peter's black hair has now changed its color. Gray has taken its place. The memories are not forgotten. They come and go. Somewhere on the edge of town, at school, fate offered him an angel. An angel with blond hair and blue eyes. Youthful with a white page when his heart felt the first glimmers of love. Of first love. The love that does not fade with time, and the winds and storms of life do not extinguish its flame.

Peter has not seen Anthea again after their separation. She left. He stayed. His life went through many stages, but his first love did not diminish. He did not divorce her from his heart. His love for her was not gone nor did it die. It was hidden in a corner of his heart, awaiting to be awaken.

His first love left him. A second love came to replace the first. A second blonde angel reminded him of the first. The second angel also left. The middle-aged man in love stayed there with another love to fight with in his tumultuous sea. Some days its waves were stormy, some days its waves were calm, but all those days created the years of his life.

The young Jewish girl left far from home to allow her wounded heart to heal. She did not see a cardiologist to heal her trauma. She traveled the world with no avail. Nowhere, nothing, and no one helped heal this deep wound. She remained incurable and disabled, hoping to find the killer again to pull the knife out of her wound. The killer who stabbed her so easily and killed the heart of her first love.

Anthea returned to her homeland, the place of her birth. The same place where her heart was terminally wounded. She wishes to meet him, her murderer, the killer of her heart. She wants to see him again. A lot of time has passed since then. Time has changed the form of the living and erased the forms of the dead. Her parents died. Her brothers emigrated. She is alone on her return. Alone in her familiar place. Nobody to welcome her back.

So she returned to New York with hope in her heart that she will once again find the murderer of her heart. She still loves him. There has been no other. Her then young classmate, Peter, that loved her with so much passion. He wanted to marry her so as not to lose her. But soon enough his passion was gone. Blown away with the wind. He let her go. He forgot her.

But she was wrong he did not forget her. His first love remained sleeping in his heart and mind, but not dead. Every so often this love would be awaken from its slumber. Again, tired, it would close its eyes and go back to sleep.

Anthea, whose first love has been alive in her heart without interruptions all these many years, settled into a hotel room in Manhattan. She knows where to start her search for her beloved. She took the train and headed for Astoria. There in the Greek corner of Astoria, Ditmars, she will find the friend she never lost. She asked around and learned that Peter still lived there. She found his home. Found out that he is married with children. Peter inherited his father's restaurant, and he still works there. His parents have died.

The door of the restaurant opened. A beautiful woman with blond hair and blue eyes, enters. At the register, a man with gray temples sits in his chair and two customers in front of him pay their bill. The young and beautiful waitress welcomes and directs the unknown customer to the table she has prepared for her.

Anthea sat in her seat. Her gaze was fixed on the man who was at the cash register. His age seems to be the same as hers. Her heart was beating fast, almost ready to break through her chest. Her unforgettable lover. Peter, near her. A little changed but not much. She is sure who he is.

Peter left the seat of his chair. He passed in front of the unknown patron. His gaze met hers intently. He stopped. He looked at her again. He noticed her blonde hair and the blue seas of her eyes. The beauty of her face. None of this has changed since then. He remembered her.

"Anthea!" His voice became loud and in the form of a shout. "Are you Anthea?" "Yes. Peter, my love. I am." "My God, is it true? Or is it a dream?" Anthea jumped up from her seat. Their hug was warm with the same passion, the same flame as in the past. "How many years... Do you remember, Anthea?" "I remember, Peter." There were few people in the hall. They did not notice the scene. The waiters understood from the smiling and happy face of their employer that some old acquaintance came to meet him.

Peter said something to Mr. John, his confidant. He hugged his beloved and they went out. The couple in love quickly left the Bronx for Manhattan in Peter's car. They arrived at the hotel. In Anthea's room they hugged again. The warm hug set their bodies on fire as the union did during their youth.

"I love you, Anthea." "You love me, Peter. Now you love me. Now you remember me. Where have you been for so many years? Where did your great love that we lived through then at school go? With the first difficulty you forgot me! Your love was like a balloon full of air. Someone punctured the balloon, and the air has since gone. With it your great love."

"I know, Anthea. It was not my fault." "I know. My love. It was not your fault. How could it be your fault? You were a child who did not have the strength to support himself. It was only his own way because you could not make your own choice."

"Who do you mean? My father?" "Yes, your father. Who, when he learned that I do not share your religion, planted a bomb in the foundations of our first love and blew it up." "I know. He was the killer of our love. I will never forgive him. I am sorry. And I am sorry for all the years that have been lost not having you in my life."

How sorry I am
the years that were lost
without having you
for so long.

I met many loves,
I loved and lost
but wherever I went
I looked for you.

Stay close to me now
my sweet love.
For I am afraid
maybe one day I will lose you.
But to forget you
I will never be able to.

Stay close to me
my sweet love.
I want to tell you again
how if one day I lose you
I will never forget you
because I will always love you.

"Listen. Peter. You have to admit that your love for me was not a strong love. It did not have deep roots. You easily forgot me. You were attracted to other loves. But my love for you had and still has roots deep in my soul. I did not forget you. You were always on my mind. My feet did not stumble on the steps. I did not lose my balance. I did not fall out of love."

"I believe you, my love. Now that I have found you again, my first love has come back to life. I will always have you near me." "How can I always be near you? Did you forget that you are married and have children? What will become of all of them? What will you do with them? Will you forget them for my sake?"

"Yes, my love. I will forget them." Peter glanced at his watch. The time had passed. "I have to leave, Anthea. Stay here. I will be back tomorrow, at the same time. Wait for me." A hasty hug and the lovers swore to meet again the next day to deal with this undying flame consuming their body and soul.

Peter ran as fast as he could to the store. He was afraid that his wife would call him, and she would not find him there. He had spoken to Mr. John to cover for him, but again he was worried. His heart settled when his confidant told him that his wife did not call. Since his excited outburst he confessed to his existing and trusted confidant about all and asked if he could justify his absence in case of an unexpected visit from his wife. He agreed.

Night finally fell and he returned home. His wife welcomed him in the same way she has as of late. With a happy and welcoming hug. She is now sure that her husband has found the right path that only leads to his family and to his family only.

And so the double life of a good family man starts now. He uses all his strength to be able to withstand the road ahead which now has two directions and many thorns. He tries to play his role as naturally as he can, so he does not arouse suspicion. And for the time being he succeeds. The next day at the same time he was in his mistress's room. The same passion. The same flame as the day before.

"Peter. This is not the situation I was hoping for. I cannot bear to see you only in secret and isolation. I cannot bear not to have you by my side again without interruption." "Anthea. Give me time. I need time. Everything will be fixed. And very quickly indeed." "I'll wait."

Peter left quickly for restaurant. He returned at night again to his house and to his smiling and trusting wife. "Helen did not notice any difference, so no damage has been done," thought Peter. The next day, after he went to work, he took care through a real estate agency and found a one- bedroom apartment in a large building in the Bronx. Very close to the restaurant. He then left very quickly for the hotel in Manhattan. Paid the bill. He took his love with him and settled her in the apartment he rented for her. Very convenient for the many daily visits of the incurable lover.

"When will I meet your wife? Your children? Why don't you invite me to your house?"

"No, my love. No, I cannot. What will I tell them? How do I explain you? I must tell them who you are and when I met you. No, no, no, not yet." "But why? What is the problem? Why can't you tell them the truth? We met at school. We were classmates once. In the same class."

"I agree but that is not the problem. There is another problem, a more serious problem."

"What is this other serious problem?" "I cannot tell you." "You cannot? Ah No! We are not doing well here at all. Are we going to have secrets between us? Do you want that? Well! You will not leave here until you tell me what your problem is." "I do not want to tell you. It is a family problem."

"A family problem. The man standing here has family problems and he keeps them secret from his mistress. Do I have a relationship with a troubled family man? Will I play the role of his therapist?" "My love, please listen to me. Do you want to see me again? Do you want not to lose me? If you want that, then believe and do not seek, as the Gospel says."

"No, my love. I do not believe and do not follow your Orthodox gospels. I want to know now, immediately, what is this family problem. A family problem so 'horrible,' that you are now showing so much fear and reservation. You have chosen to hide."

"Okay. I will tell you: My wife is a very jealous woman. This is my big family problem. She cannot and does not want to see me with any woman, ever. She does not tolerate seeing me talk to a woman. She does not understand and does not distinguish if I met this woman now or someone from my past."

He continues. "If she knows you, she will do everything in her power to make you disappear. Not to kill you, but to kill me, she would not let me see you again. She killed me many times over the years. I am finally completely resurrected now. I want to live once again. Life is so beautiful now that I found you again. Do you want her to find a reason to kill me again? No. I do not want that. This time I want to live my life as it was meant to be. And I will live only for you."

"My love, I feel sorry for you. Your problem is a really big one. You were correct." "That is why I did not want to talk about it. It is too painful but more so, she is my wife. I must not expose her bad behaviors. I do not want to blame anyone for my misfortune. You forced me to tell you."

"Sorry, Peter. I never imagined such a thing would have happened to you. Do not forget ever. You are not alone. This is not an unusual problem in relationships, marriages. Usually sixty percent of couples have the same problem. All you have left that you can do is patience. So be patient until you see what will happen. But I want to meet this lady. Tell me where and how. Please. I want to see her. Even from a distance. Maybe come to the restaurant when you bring her there and I will pretend to be the indifferent patron that you do not know?"

"No. No, I do not want you to come back to the restaurant. Everyone there saw you and noticed our behavior towards each other and all our many hugs. How can I pretend now that I do not know you? They will assume I am hiding something, and that assumption will feed gossip."

"Then where else?" "I will find a way and tell you. Let me think about it. I must be going now. I'll see you again tomorrow." The next day, Peter found himself in Anthea's apartment at the same time. "Well, my love, what do you think? Where and when will I be able to see this woman who oppresses you? I am starting to dislike her before I even meet her."

"On Sunday at around noon. Can you be in Astoria Park? There you will see my wife. You will meet her because she will be with me. My children will also be with me. I will pretend that I do not know you. You must do the same. You do not know me. You will walk indifferently. I will too. I will make sure we sit on a bench that has another next to it. If you sit on the next bench, you will see my wife better up close. Okay? Is this what you want? Are you happy?" "Yes. I'm happy." "I still cannot understand why you want to see her. What does this have to do with us?"

"I wish to see what she is like with you and the children? I want to understand what kind of person she is. I know you will not understand such a thing. I want to see her face, hear her talking to you, see if she hugs and holds you and how you show love to her. I want to understand your relationship with your wife and children." "Okay. I'm going to fold. So on Sunday. Do you agree?" "Agreed."

The lovers swore to meet again the next day. Their love is strong. It continues to grow as time goes on. They need to see each other. Otherwise the heart aches and suffers. Peter at home in the evenings. Tired, but also interested in his family. His role in this theater is doing well. His wife does not suspect what is happening behind her back. On Sunday, the guilty husband takes the unsuspecting wife in his arms and goes for a walk in the park with their children.

They sat on the bench he had chosen. Children play on the grass. The mistress was not long in coming. She sat on the next bench. She was lucky. The bench next to them was empty. Peter purposely did not turn his head to see the woman sitting next to him. Absolutely indifferent. The actors are doing well. The wife glanced next to her. The mistress retaliated. Their eyes met. The recognition was made. The mistress got up. She glanced at the children once again and disappeared.

The next day the couple met in the apartment of the mistress. "Your wife is so very beautiful. I did not expect to see such beauty and elegance. I thought she would be unattractive because she envies you so much. But she is more beautiful than you. I cannot understand why she envies you. You should envy her."

"I know. Whether she is beautiful or unattractive, it does not matter. She is infected with the disease of jealousy and can never be cured. I am the victim here. I will never untangle myself from this future." "You can untangle yourself. You must really want to do so." "What do you mean?"

"Get a divorce and move on with everything else. I understand your current situation. What can you do when it is tyrannical? I came here because I love you and I want to have you as my husband. In order for this to happen, your wife must leave from your life. You cannot have two wives simultaneously. I am unnecessary. You can give me up."

"Do not ever repeat what you said. I cannot and will not live without you. I will never let you go."

"Then do something about it." "Okay. I promise. I will see what I can do. But you must see that my children are in the middle."

"Children, yes, children. You are not the only one who has children and divorces. Do not try to find excuses. Except if maybe I am not that important to you. I tell you again this. You do not need me very much. You only have me around as an appetizer added onto your daily intake of food."

"No! No. No. You are my main dish. Without you I will be lost."

"Then what are you waiting for? Go forward with our plans. I cannot play a secondary role in your life. I want to be your first choice for you wife. Otherwise you will lose me for the second time and forever this time." "Anthea. Please. Do not do this to me." "Then do what you must do now. Today. Not tomorrow. If you do not want to lose me." "All right. I will begin the process of getting a divorce." "Good. I will wait."

Peter has a dilemma. What to do? In front of him a steep cliff and behind him a cool running stream. He loves his wife, despite her flaws. He married her because he was in love with her. Everything is so much better between them. Life is peaceful and loving. Then there are the children. He loves and adores his children. Can he destroy his family's happiness just to obtain his own personal happiness? Are they at fault for their parents' stupidity? After all these years of misery and uncertainty for his children, he is finally giving them a stable life. They are innocent bystanders whose life he was about to destroy. Why should they lose everything that they know?

In their next meetings, the two lovers have the same questions and answers: "Did you start the process needed for your divorce?" "Yes, of course I started. I instructed my lawyer to begin the proceedings." "Nice. Finally you broke away from your childish character. You have become a man." In fact, Peter did not make any move whatsoever. He did not even hire a lawyer. No divorce proceedings.

He just cannot do this. He continues to lie to his mistress just to keep her in his life. He just cannot run away from either his family or his mistress. He understands that he is being self-destructive in continuing this illicit affair. He sees in front of him a labyrinth of lies followed by a steep cliff. But he does not want to back down from running towards this end. He does not want to be saved. Without his beloved, death is preferable.

The meetings continue, many times a day. No time is wasted because the place of sin is right next door. Very close to the restaurant. The wife calls her husband. Most of the time she finds him at work. When she does not find him there, his confidant reassures her: "He just left. He is out to buy supplies for the restaurant ."

The mistress is locked in her apartment. She waits for her lover with the anticipation of a blond colored butterfly flying to attach to her flower to taste its honey. The mistress does not work anywhere. Her lover has taken care of all her financial needs. She has him during the days but does not have him at night. Their daily meetings are fleeting and most of the time fast. Night meetings do not exist. The heat of those daily meetings must last until the morning when their heat renews once again. The lover with the blond hair and the blue eyes is looking forward to these hugs becoming night hugs.

"Peter. My love. I am bored. I am tired. How much longer will I wait? When will you finally be free? I want you to be mine, only mine. I want you at night. Not only during the day."

"I told you. I will take care of it and for now we must wait for results from my lawyer." "Yes, but so far, I do not see any results. At least why do you not want to stay with me overnight in my apartment? Tonight, just for tonight."

"No. My love. It is not possible. If I do not go to my home at night, what will I say to my wife? Where will I say that I was?" "Find an excuse. Like you went to Canada for example. Tell her that you are looking to find someone who owes you money. When will you break free from your wife's cold embrace?" "No. I never had to break free, because I had no reason to do so." "Now do you not have a reason. I want to know." "Now I have reasons. I want to, but I cannot satisfy your demand right now. Everything will become complicated if I make such a move. Why are you in such a hurry? Have a little patience. When I have my divorce, I will be all yours." "Okay. I will be patient. Let us see when this will finally happen."

Helen, Peter's wife, is no longer worried for she is sure her husband has found his way home as far as she was concerned. Her illness was under control. She took the opportunity to change her life and she did. Yet she longed for her island, the place, and its inhabitants. Born in a warm and sun filled place, she could not stand the clouds and the cold of the inhospitable land where she lives and calls home. "Peter, what would you say about a trip this summer to Cyprus? Let us all go together."

"Helen, you know I cannot get away from here at this time. The restaurant is not doing well. I have to attract more patrons. Many other restaurants that have opened around us, even at our Manhattan location and have taken patrons from us." "That is not a problem at all. Since you cannot come, I will take the children and go there for a month. Are you okay with that idea?"

"My love, of course I agree. It is your homeland. You have the right to miss it and wish to visit it. Stay there as long as you want. Even more than a month if you wish. Do not worry about me, I will do fine on my own. Of course I will miss you and the children very much, but I will wait here patiently until you return."

Peter rejoiced but did not show it. This was exactly what he needed and wanted, to be free to enjoy his crazy love with no other obligations or interruptions. In one month's time the wife and the children were at the airport. The impatient husband took them there to insure they left. He said goodbye and the plane left.

The mistress's wish to enjoy his hugs throughout the night came true. She was offered this opportunity by the ignorance and trust of a wife, who was convinced that her husband finally became a faithful husband. The lovers are eagerly awaiting their time together. That same night in the empty house of the unfaithful husband, their bodies became one. The schedule now changed. The daytime hasty rendezvous became long nightly ones.

In the family home there were concerns. And as in all neighborhoods, people are curious and want to know what is going on in the house next door. The head of the family in love knows of this possibility and took action. Safety measures were taken by those around him. His mistress comes late at night into his house and leaves with him in the very early hours of the morning. The wife calls her husband every day and finds him at work devoted to the execution of his employer's duties. She also calls in the early evening at home and finds him there alone, nostalgic for his wife and children.

She feels sorry for him and feels bad that he was left alone in an empty house. But the unfaithful husband reassures her that everything is fine. Of course he is missing them, but what matters is that they are having a good time there on this beautiful island. And even if they want to stay all summer, he is fine with it. For himself he told his wife not to be upset. His hours are spent happily at his restaurant.

Lucky was the unfaithful husband as everything fell into place. He anxiously awaits his wife's answer, will she stay on the island all summer. And the answer came after a very short delay because the wife was concerned about the unfairness of leaving her husband alone for so long. But since he seems okay with it and since it is so nice there and the children are excited to be there, she decided to accept and stay in Cyprus all summer.

While Helen was in Cyprus, she thought of meeting her friends Stavros and Maria, who had been their neighbors and best friends several years ago. More so she missed her girlfriend, Maria. She wanted to announce the good news to her how her husband had changed and how they now live a good family life. She searched and soon enough found them. They are not far from the village and her brother's house. Their meeting was a happy one. They remembered their life in America. Their good and bad days together.

"What is Peter doing? Why didn't he come with you?" Stauros asks. "He wanted to come, but he has problems with the restaurant. Things are not going so well. You know how hands on he is. He wants everything to be perfect." "You, Stavros, what are you doing now? Are you working?"

"Sure. I was assigned to the Town's Municipality office. We are doing fine. We live in paradise. This is the life. Sun, sea, and clean air. All in our homeland. What else can we want?"

"All I can say is that I am very jealous of your wonderful life. I cannot say anything else."

Their friends hosted Helen and her children in their house for two days. They eat wonderful meals, sleep for a few hours, a siesta from noon until afternoon. Party at night in nightclubs. Nice life. How she misses this! May she never return back to the land of Christopher Columbus. If only she could do what Stauros and Maria did. If she was able to get her husband to leave America and live with her here in her homeland. On this beautiful island. In the paradise made by God. Will she be able to make such a dream come true?

She does not believe she could. She rules it out. Peter was born in America. That is his homeland. No one leaves their own place of birth so easily. But she will try. Maybe she can do it. The life they live there is not a life. It is a type of hell. And his restaurant that he has become a slave to, how will we get rid of it? This thought took over her brain. She will do everything she can to make her plan succeed. Now is the time to think of how best to convince him to come and live permanently in Cyprus.

That is why in her phone calls she praises the beauty of the island and the life of its people. But he does not pay much attention to the conversation which is directed at him to convince him of the attributes of this island. On the contrary, he is glad that his wife likes her stay there and can stay as long as possible. If possible, forever. He does not need her any longer. He has found his first and true love. He now lives in another's embrace. He is flying high amongst the clouds with his feet off the ground.

Helen realized that the proposals she offered to her husband were being dismissed. His thoughts were aimed elsewhere, and elsewhere they ended up. Her husband has a nice life where he is. He is not interested in moving to a foreign land. But a bell rang in her ears once again: Why does her beloved husband urge her to stay even longer in her homeland? Is he not missing her? Does he not miss the presence of his children? Is there anything else she does not know? But again, why should there be something else, someone else? Even from a distance, she is spying on her husband's life. On her phone she finds him at work during the day. She finds him at home in the evening. No, her husband cannot do what he once did. Now she made up her mind. She is happy. Peter loves her. She is sure of that. So she decided to stay on her beautiful island until the end of August.

CHAPTER SEVEN: PETER AND HELEN'S FINAL CHAPTER

Three months from June until the end of August the illicit couple live in their own created paradise, without prisons and chains. They have complete freedom to fly amongst the clouds on the wings of love. The first and possibly the "last" love for Peter. By day in the mistress's apartment. By night at the house of the unfaithful husband. Two revolving doors in his life. The life of all mortals of this world is short. Time flies. Most do not manage to enjoy such joys. The few, who have the luck to do so, are filled with the joy of its beauties.

The unfaithful man between two loves. He cannot walk the same path for both. One is totally separate from the other. They cannot exist simultaneously. In order for one to live, the other must die. The mistress is the moral perpetrator of the murder of the wife. She is pushing him into committing this crime. To kill the legal spouse. To eliminate her rival. She places the ax in his hand. He cannot lift it. The ax is too heavy. He cannot pick it up. The unfaithful man cannot kill. He cannot decide who will live and who will die. He wants both loves in his life. He loves both of them and cannot chose.

The last month of summer is August. With the end of this month, the paradise of the couple ends. Hell awaits both of them. It will open its mouth to swallow them. The flames will engross them. They feel the fire next to them. They resist and fight the inevitable. Still standing on the edge of the abyss. They struggle to escape, holding hands and hoping not to fall.

The missing spouse gathers her belongings from her place to return to the "faithful" embrace of her husband, who is left "alone" away from her and waits for her return. She feels sorry for him. She feels guilty and selfish. She should not have done what she did. To reward herself for not caring about her partner who claims to love her. They should have decided to travel together. As much as he did not want to, she should have insisted. In the end she would succeed. Repentant, she returns to her beloved man, who is waiting for her. In one more day she will be seeing him again at their home in America. In New York. In Astoria. In Ditmars. Under the big bridge that covers them and protects them from lightning.

Last night, in the mistress' apartment at this time. The next day the arrival of the legal spouse. The lawful couple's house should have no signs of sinful use. The "unfaithful" couple, who is waiting for the unsuspecting wife, cleaned it and sprinkled it with cleaners to kill the germs. "Your wife is coming tomorrow. What are you going to do? Will you talk to her?" "Yes. I will talk to her." "This is your last chance. There will be no other. If you do nothing, we are done. You will never see me again."

"My love. I told you; I will talk to her. Everything will be fine. You will see. This is not the end of our great love. And you will see me again and I will see you again." "I do not believe you. A premonition tells me that I will not see you again. Stay with me tonight. Do not leave."

Tonight is more for us
The last of nights
Tonight stay until morning
and be close to me.

Tomorrow of our separation
the day dawns.
And our star crossed love
tonight will end.

I will lose you before dawn
So for tonight hold me
In your arms and let me
lean on you like a falling willow.

As the train whistle blows
I feel the daggers been thrown
To create a hole in my heart.

Time does not stop for us
and the words you say to me tonight
the dawn will carry them away.

My tears are flowing
From afar another love is coming
To erase me from your heart.
Stop the night
if for a moment
For by dawn
My love will die.

I wish for lightening
In the night
Let its shadow cover my sight
So I no longer can see.

My love let us cry
Together as one
And keep on crying
When the night is done.

What we once had
Hold close to
To our heart
But let us live on.

The lover left his mistress's nest. He returned to his house. He sat in the yard. The night spreads its black wings. The moon above illuminates the streets and the houses. The sinner raised his head to the sky to see the stars covered by the clouds. He is looking to find his life. His life that is blown by the wind.

*My whole life
is a responsibility.
He takes all from me
And gives me nothing.*

*My whole life
is a furnace
who has thrown me in
and is simmering me.*

*My whole life
is nonsense
with neither purpose
nor meaning.*

*My whole life
is a cigarette
I do not like it
and yet I smoke it.*

Yes. The life of man, sitting in the yard of his house, under the black sky, was not and is not his life. Others control it and others own it. He was born this way. And so it continues this way. He does not direct his steps alone. He waits for the instructions of others to show him the way. He has two loves; they have placed him in the middle. They are holding him captive. One pushes him to kill the other. And he must commit the crime.

It is past midnight. The desperate man got up from the seat in the yard. He entered his house. He lay down on his bed. The weight of his head is pronounced. Sleep does not help him feel relieved. Thoughts stop him from relaxing. Tomorrow his other love returns. The one that must disappear. What will he do? Can he commit murder? He does not know...

He does not know what to do this desperate man. He cannot kill. Life is a gift from God. Only God can remove it from the mortals of the earth, which he created. Only God will decide his own life, which fate has abused. His life now feels like it is ending.

> *"A car with two horses*
> *bring my eyes to a close.*
> *In life with its twists and turns*
> *It is the rider's time to lead.*
>
> *One horse should be white,*
> *like the dreams I had as a child.*
> *The other horse should be black*
> *like my own dark ill-fated life."*

The light of day illuminates his thoughts. His decision has been made. He must act before others change the road he must take. At the end of the road only a dead end. It leads nowhere. But a bridge slightly down the road opened her arms to him. She will save him. She will open the closed passage to him found on the opposite side of the drowning river.

It was late. It was night. It is raining outside. Peter is ready to leave. He picked up his umbrella. He closed the door of his house and started walking. The bridge straight ahead was calling him. He is going to meet her soon. He walked. He arrived. He started climbing the stairs that lead him to her arms. He reached the top of the bridge. His hands gripped the iron railings. The black water of the river reflects the colorful lights that illuminate all around. He stood between the railings with the closed umbrella in his hand. He bowed his head. He looked down. The water of the river is black, dark, it scares him. In his ears the voice of the mistress.

"This is the last chance for you, if you do not talk to her and proceed to divorce your wife, I will leave, and you will never see me again." "No." He thought. "I prefer death to losing my first love. My wife is coming tomorrow. I will not talk to her. I cannot. But if I do not talk to her, my first love will be gone forever. No, I do not want to lose her. It will be better for me to die."

In his imagination a vivid image of his first love. She is standing in front of him. It prevents him from leaving.

"Let me go, my love.
You set this course for me.
You, my sweet sin.

Your kisses and caresses
that you gave me in the evenings
they shook my soul and my peace.

I surrendered to you.
I did not account to anyone.
Now whatever she wants, let it be done.

How it happened I do not know.
I only know that I now suffer
to ask, to imagine,
your illegal kisses
now that I will leave
and I say goodbye to you ."

He looked at the water again. A magnet seemed to be pulling his body to the bottom. He raised his head. He looked at the sky, the moon near its sunset. She is waiting for him so they can leave together. He stretches the body. Looks at the sky once again. A lightning illuminated the darkness. A loud cry in the air: "Goodnight, Life." It was his own cry.

He opened the palm of his hand. The umbrella is now gone.

It falls like a fireball into the water. He opened the palm of his other hand, which was holding the railings. His heavy body hit the canopy and black water under the bridge. A big jet of water rose and sucked the body of the desperate and determined under. The body of the one who had two great loves and was stuck in the middle.

The body of the one who could not live with one love, without the other. The body of Peter. The owner of the restaurant in the Bronx. Peter, who was waiting for his wife to return the next day from her trip. To carry out the order of the mistress. Dilemma with a deadlock. Above the bridge he stood. Down in the river he now belongs. The solution was diving into the cold and dark waters below and finally death.

Helen and the children are still in Cyprus, ready to return back to America. Every now and then she calls her husband. She found him both at home and at work. One day before her departure she called home. She did not find him there. She called the restaurant. Mr. John told her that he did not appear there all day. He does not know where he is. The wife was worried. She left on her trip in despair.

She arrived at Kennedy Airport. She called home. No answer. She called his work. She did not find him there either. She chose to wait at the airport for an hour, hoping he would come to get her. Peter knew the day and the hour that they were coming. But he did not appear. She despaired. After a long wait she called the taxi.

She came in with her children. She arrived at her house. She opened the closed door with her keys. No one was inside. Anxiety in her soul. Where is her husband? Her body is trembling. Her heart is slowly beating. She feels an extreme sense of sadness. She proceeds to lie down on the couch. The children are helping.

The neighbors run in willing to help search for him. Until yesterday, the lights seemed on inside the house. So someone would have been inside. Many times they saw and talked to their neighbor. They know he is busy. He always came late and always left early. They suggested to her that maybe he had to go somewhere for work issues. They tried to help her relax.

Helen cannot take it anymore as time passes. An accident must have happened to her husband. But how? By car? The car is in the garage intact. No. It cannot be an accident. Maybe someone killed him. But, if so, where is the corpse? Now, she is sure. He was kidnapped by criminals, and they want ransom to free him. Maybe they know she is coming home today. Her husband might have told them about her. They will call her to give them the money.

She thought of notifying the police. But suddenly stopped the call. The case can be complicated. Better to wait. All night long next to the phone waiting to hear the voices of the kidnappers. No phone calls. The phone was mute. It has dawned. In her mind another thought that excludes abduction. Probably something else is happening. Does her husband have an involvement with organized crime? If so, maybe the mobsters have him, and they have killed him?

The issue is serious. She understood it and was scared. Her husband was killed. There is no other explanation to justify his sudden disappearance. She feels she is losing her mind. With a trembling hand she grabs the handset. She is calling Mr. John to come to the house quickly. He must know. He cannot help but know what has happened.

In just under an hour the trusted employee arrived. From the explanations he gave her, she was not able to obtain any useful information. Her conclusion, Mr. John knows nothing. Peter never spoke to him about anything regarding his private life. Of course he did hid his boss's confidential confession about the blonde mistress. He thought that his boss's disappearance may be related to her. She could have taken him and flown him to other ports and other places. He preferred to keep quiet about this possibility, for now keep his mouth shut.

The desperate wife could not wait any longer, she alerted the police. The police undertook the investigation. The disappearance of the well-known businessman in the suburbs of New York City became the topic of the day. Televisions and radios could not stop repeating the event in their news.

The mistress has not seen her lover for two days. She knew that his wife would return the day before. She was worried when she had no news. Today she hears the news of his disappearance from the media. She is upset, but again she thinks that nothing bad is happening. She has known her boyfriend since his youth. He is easily frightened, a cowardly man. It is part of his personality. He is probably too afraid to confront his wife and tell her about the divorce. That is all that could have happened. Somewhere the idiot is hiding.

But the days go by. Peter does not appear. Neither alive nor dead. What is going on? The thought that the case is a crime is slowly crystallizing. Neighbors and friends. Known and unknown assist the police in their investigation. A week of intensive effort without results. Police continued their investigations throughout the district. Even outside of it. In other states.

It is the beginning of the second week of Peter's disappearance. A little further down the bridge at one end of the river, a corpse washed up, tangled between dry tree branches. The police were notified. The body was exhumed and taken to the morgue. They called the wife, who was looking for her missing husband, for identification. Helen arrived at the police station with a tight heart and then was taken to the morgue. They uncovered the corpse. At the sight of the corpse, the upset wife immediately recognized her beloved partner. She collapsed into the arms of her companions.

From this moment on the great drama begins. When Helen saw her husband's face deformed and swollen by apparent drowning, she lost her mind. She was taken to the hospital. She was never well again. She had a complete mental breakdown and was hospitalized for an indefinite period of time. The neighbors took the children to their home. They notified her brother in Cyprus. The brother came with his wife. They stayed at his sister's house with the unfortunate children.

The medical examiner issued his conclusion. Death came from drowning. It excludes any other cause. The body does not show any injury, except for a black mark swollen on the temple which indicates that the body fell with its head in the water and the pressure of the water caused the injury. Maybe the man wanted to commit suicide. Maybe someone pushed him off the bridge. The cause of his fall was inconclusive. He did fall from the bridge. This is proven by the examination of the body. The man fell into the water from a great height, with the consequence of drowning.

The sick woman remains at a clinic in Manhattan. She did not attend the funeral for her husband in St. Demetrius Church in Astoria. Friends and neighbors with the brother were there. They all accompanied the coffin to the Flushing cemetery. In the crowd a well-known stranger with a black handkerchief around her blond hair and big black glasses covering her eyes and her tears.

She approached the coffin, which inside held her lover, at the time of farewell, and placed her last goodbye on it: A crimson rose soaked in tears. Then she ran away. She arrived at her house. As she approached her door she fell. Neighbors took her to the hospital. Very little time passed, and she was pronounced dead. Her heart could not handle the loss. It was Anthea. Peter's first love. The mistress who felt his death, not unlike his wife. She left with him. Both are now free to continue their great love in the clouds near the sky and in the light.

A month later the brother took his sick sister, along with the children, and they left for Cyprus. The woman was locked up in a mental hospital. The brother took the children and made them his own. He did not have his own children. The children were finally in a happy family and found the peace they longed for.

This is the end of our drama, which was caused by two incurable diseases that lead to a sickness of the soul. The infidelity of a husband and the jealousy of a wife. Jealousy created out of an excessive and controlling love. Incurable diseases that had their toll over time. The end being one of death and madness. These diseases infected this unfortunate couple here and caused death in the husband first followed immediately by madness in the wife.

Beware such ailments!!